EVERYONE IS TALKING ABOUT
NERDS!

"Funny, clever, and thoroughly entertaining."
—SCHOOL LIBRARY JOURNAL

"This fun adventure is sure to attract followers, who will look forward to the sequels. . . . Beavers's comic strip–style illustrations add further appeal."
—BOOKLIST

"The inventive details, story, and made-up futuristic technology will keep pages turning."
—KIRKUS REVIEWS

"A charming and funny tale of underdogs saving the day."
—PUBLISHERS WEEKLY

"Deeply funny."
—INSTRUCTOR MAGAZINE

"*NERDS* is a fun middle-grade romp, with a great multicultural cast. . . . [It] gives the geeks and underdogs of the world a chance to shine, and that's something this current Braceface is glad to see."
—KIDLITERATE BLOG

BY MICHAEL BUCKLEY

The Sisters Grimm

NERDS

NERDS

ATTACK OF THE BULLIES

• BOOK FIVE •

MICHAEL BUCKLEY

Illustrations by
ETHEN BEAVERS

AMULET BOOKS

NEW YORK

The Library of Congress has catalogued the hardcover edition of this book as follows:

Buckley, Michael, 1969–
Attack of the bullies / by Michael Buckley ; illustrations by Ethen Beavers.
pages cm. — (NERDS ; book five)
Summary: When Miss Information kidnaps the President's daughter, it is up to twelve-year-old Ruby, also known as Pufferfish, to use her super-nanobyte-enhanced allergies in leading the NERDS' investigation.
ISBN 978-1-4197-0857-2 (hardback)
[1. Superheroes—Fiction. 2. Spies—Fiction. 3. Kidnapping—Fiction.
4. Time travel—Fiction. 5. Bullies—Fiction. 6. Presidents—Family—Fiction.
7. Humorous stories.] I. Title.
PZ7.B882323Att 2013
[Fic]—dc23
2013015981

ISBN for this edition: 978-1-4197-1222-7

Text copyright © 2013 Michael Buckley
Illustrations copyright © 2013 Ethen Beavers
Book design by Chad W. Beckerman

Printed and bound in U.S.A.
10 9 8 7 6 5 4 3 2 1

Amulet Books are available at special discounts when purchased in quantity for premiums and promotions as well as fundraising or educational use. Special editions can also be created to specification. For details, contact specialsales@abramsbooks.com or the address below.

ABRAMS
THE ART OF BOOKS SINCE 1949

115 West 18th Street
New York, NY 10011
www.abramsbooks.com

For Jason Wells—
always managing to
control the chaos

Prologue

The principal of Thomas Knowlton Middle School was working at his desk when the ninjas attacked. They wore black masks and held sharp swords over their heads. One crashed through the door with a high-pitched wail, his deadly weapon slicing the air, but he was stopped in his tracks when the principal karate-chopped him in the Adam's apple. *Ouch!* Another ninja climbed through the window, but his head was crushed when the principal slammed it shut *Oof!* A third ninja dropped from an air duct in the ceiling. His nunchucks swirled in deadly arcs, wrapping around the principal's beefy forearm. But that was a mistake the ninja would forever regret, because the principal used the nunchucks to yank the ninja forward for a skull-splitting head butt. *Lights out!*

When it looked like the attack was over, two more ninjas popped out of the drawers of a steel file cabinet and attacked using their fists and feet, knocking the principal backward onto his desk. They held him down and, chuckling arrogantly, removed gleaming daggers from the folds of their clothes. But the principal was trained in several martial arts and highly proficient in the monkey, snake, and crane fighting styles. Plus, he was Irish, so he knew his way around a street fight. He snatched a stapler off his desk and slammed it into one ninja's forehead and then the other's. Both men cried out in agony and stumbled backward, onto the bodies of their fallen brothers.

The principal stood over the pile of broken villains. Then he started to applaud. "Thanks, guys," he said.

"Yeah, yeah . . . ," the men groaned as they staggered to their feet.

One of the ninjas took off his mask, revealing a chubby face and a large bald spot in the center of his curly brown hair. He didn't look like a ninja. He looked like an accountant.

"Did we at least surprise you this time?" he groused.

The principal nodded. "Absolutely, Randy. I was completely taken off guard. I didn't see the file cabinet thing coming at all. That was a nice touch."

"He's just saying that because he doesn't want to hurt our

feelings," another ninja groaned. Underneath his mask he had bright red hair and a face full of freckles.

"No, Barry. I really was intimidated."

Randy shook his head. "I don't know why you want us to do this, anyway. You're the boss now. Your biggest fear should be getting a paper cut or someone parking in your designated space. Why keep training?"

"You don't actually miss your old job, do you?" Barry asked.

"Miss my old job? No! That's ridiculous. Why would I miss it?"

"I have no idea," Randy said. "It was humiliating. You're a decorated war hero, and they put you in that stupid school kitchen with the hairnet and the Tater Tots. What a waste! This promotion was long overdue. You *deserve* to be director of the National Espionage, Rescue, and Defense Society, so take it easy."

"Thanks for the pep talk, guys, but I'm fine," the principal said. "I've got to get back to work. See you next week?"

"Not if we see you first," Barry said as he slunk out the window.

The others vanished through the air ducts and into the filing cabinet. In the blink of an eye they were gone.

The principal put the upended coatrack back in its place,

38°52' N, 77°0' E

adjusted his portrait of the president of the United States on the wall, and gathered what was left of his office supplies.

He looked at the stack of paperwork on his desk and sighed. Truth was, he didn't know how to take it easy. He did miss the adventure of the field. There was nothing as satisfying as the sound of a bad guy's nose breaking beneath his fist. But what he really missed was . . . well, if anyone found out, he would be the laughing stock of the espionage community. He crossed the room to a small file cabinet locked tight with fourteen different dead bolts. He fished seven of the keys out of his pockets, opened the hollow heel in his left shoe for another, found two in between his big toe and his second toe, and four more in a secret pocket at the base of his pant leg. When he had unlocked all the bolts, he opened the cabinet and pulled out his most prized possessions: a spatula, a pair of orthopedic sneakers, a hairnet, and a flowery smock.

He caressed them lovingly. Why was it so hard to let go of his previous job as the school's lunch lady? Why did he miss the heat lamps, corn nuggets, and fish surprise?

Suddenly, the phone rang. It wasn't the phone on his desk. It was *the* phone. He stuffed his kitchen tools back in the cabinet and raced to his desk. Underneath his coffee mug was a glowing red button. He slammed it hard with the palm of his hand and watched as his drab, poorly decorated office went through a dramatic transformation. The yellowing walls flipped over to reveal banks of computers and electronic maps of the world. His ancient, clunky desk sank into the floor and was replaced with a blinking, beeping control panel. The grimy ceiling fan collapsed in on itself, and a large television monitor took its place. The glossy black screen blinked to life and his boss, a tough-as-nails five-star general named Savage, appeared on it.

Savage's reputation as a fearless soldier made the principal's record look downright cowardly. Rumors claimed the general once got out of a pit of quicksand just by threatening it.

Now, however, Savage's massive bullet-shaped head looked sweaty and his tiny eyes shifted nervously. "Hello, Director. I wish I had time for chitchat, but we have a crisis on our hands that needs your team's attention."

"What is it, sir?"

"We have it from good sources that the president's daughter, Tessa Lipton, is about to be kidnapped."

The principal wasn't the kind of man to gasp, but the news of such a brazen crime took his breath away. "When? How? Who?"

Savage's massive head dissolved and was replaced with an image of the complete opposite: a sweet, cheerful-looking twelve-year-old girl with a grin as big as the midwestern sky. Her image morphed into a photo of an ultramodern building.

"We don't know the when or how, but we think we have a where—Sugarland Academy, a very prestigious prep school for the children of political bigwigs and power brokers. It's here in Arlington."

"I know the lunch lady over there," the principal said. "The security is top-notch."

"Did you say you know the . . . lunch lady there?" the general asked.

"Um, we used to trade recipes."

"Okaaaaay," Savage said slowly. "Anyway, Sugarland has its own twelve-officer police department that cooperates with Tessa's four-man Secret Service detail."

"That's a lot of eyeballs on one person," the principal said. "Who would even try to kidnap her?"

The image was replaced with a photo of a woman wearing a black mask with a white skull painted on it.

The principal scowled. "Ms. Holiday!"

"She's calling herself 'Miss Information' now," Savage said. "We managed to get a mole inside her organization. He called it chaotic, filled with hundreds of scientists working on thousands of schemes aimed at every corner of the world. It's really breathtaking how quickly she's put this thing together."

"And she's had us running ragged ever since," the principal growled. "I've had to split the team to handle it all. What else is this mole saying?"

"Nothing. He's dead. We found his remains in the belly of a beached great white shark this morning. We've alerted the president. He and the First Lady are beside themselves with worry. If the commander in chief's own daughter can be kidnapped, what does it say about our national security?"

The principal nodded. "This is not going to be easy for us, General. It will be tough to keep an eye on Tessa without her or the president knowing about it. The founders of this team were very concerned about staying out of the political maneuverings of whoever is running the country. If the politicians were to find out we had a superteam at their disposal, the kids' lives would be turned upside down."

"Then I suggest the kids keep their powers to themselves."

"No upgrades," the principal said. "Good idea, sir. I'll have the kids enroll at Sugarland Academy."

"I'll work with the Secret Service and the school's police," Savage said. "There is one other problem, Director. Sugarland is a sophisticated school. The students are mature and cultured."

"Sir?"

"And your kids are not—especially the hyper one."

"Flinch. Don't worry, sir. The team will rise to the occasion."

"And leave the crazy one at home."

The principal paused. Did the boss really think he would do something so dumb as send Heathcliff Hodges on a mission? If only there was somewhere to send him . . . Unfortunately, until the brains in the science department found a way to return his parents' memories of him, Heathcliff had to stay in the Playground.

"I don't think I have to tell you this mission is your top priority," Savage continued. "I know it's not easy to fill Agent Brand's shoes, but if you and the team succeed in keeping Tessa safe, no one will question your leadership."

"Is someone questioning my leadership?" the principal asked.

But the screen had already gone black. The room's technology was quickly replaced with the drab, battered furniture of his principal's office.

The principal was tempted to run to the file cabinet, snatch the spatula, and stuff it safely in the pocket of his suit jacket. It would make him feel better, but deep down he knew Randy and Barry were right. He was the boss now. He had to put the grill and the deep-fat fryer behind him.

"Take me to the Playground," he said out loud.

A green light flashed and the floor beneath him opened. It was time to fight the bad guys, and he was heading toward a place where he could do just that.

END TRANSMISSION.

KID, YOU'RE LIKE BEDBUGS:
I CAN'T GET RID OF YOU. I'VE
TRIED EVERYTHING SHORT OF DDT,
BUT YOU KEEP SHOWING UP AND
BEING ANNOYING. FIRST THERE WERE
THOSE EMBARRASSING DNA TESTS,
THEN THE CODE-BREAKING QUIZ, THEN
I THREW THAT PSYCHOLOGICAL EXAM
AT YOU, AND FINALLY THE PHYSICAL
CHALLENGES! EITHER YOU'RE
PASSIONATE ABOUT BEING A SECRET
AGENT OR YOU'RE DIM IN THE HEAD.

MY MONEY IS ON YOU BEING DIM.

SO, WHAT'S LEFT FOR YOU TO PROVE?
NOTHING.
YOU ACTUALLY MADE IT. YOU'RE A
MEMBER OF THE NATIONAL ESPIONAGE,
RESCUE, AND DEFENSE SOCIETY.
CONGRATULATIONS. WRITE
YOUR CODE NAME BELOW.

REALLY? YOU'RE GOING WITH THAT?

I MEAN, IT'S NOT EXACTLY
INTIMIDATING. IN FACT, IT'S
DOWNRIGHT SILLY. WHY NOT CALL
YOURSELF "FLUFFY BUNNY" OR "THE
CABBAGE"? HUH? MY CODE NAME?
AGENT BEANPOLE.
SHUT YOUR MOUTH!
BEANPOLE IS A FIERCE CODE NAME.
IT HAS AN AIR OF MYSTERY
ABOUT IT, TOO.
STOP LAUGHING.
I HATE YOU.
LET'S MOVE ON. MY NAME IS
MICHAEL BUCKLEY. I WAS ONCE
A MEMBER OF THE NATIONAL
ESPIONAGE, RESCUE, AND DEFENSE
SOCIETY. THESE DAYS I DOCUMENT
THEIR ADVENTURES AND
WEED OUT THE POSERS WHO
WANT TO JOIN THE TEAM.
(WELL, I TRY TO WEED THEM OUT.)

THE ORGANIZATION WAS FOUNDED IN
THE 1970S, LONG BEFORE YOU WERE
BORN. WHAT WERE THE '70S LIKE?
A-W-E-S-O-M-E! EVERYBODY DRESSED
REALLY WELL AND WE ALL HAD THESE
COOL HAIRCUTS. DON'T BELIEVE ME?
ASK YOUR PARENTS TO SHOW YOU
SOME PICTURES. I'LL WAIT.

SEE, I TOLD YOU. MAN, DO I MISS
MY BUTTERFLY COLLARS. ANYWAY,
LET'S GET STARTED. WHAT YOU'RE
HOLDING IN YOUR SWEATY HANDS IS
THE LAST NERDS FILE. AND UNLIKE
THE PREVIOUS FOUR, THERE'S NO
TEST. THIS CASE FILE IS ALL ABOUT
HISTORY. YOU'RE GOING TO GET A
GLIMPSE OF THE GREATEST
AGENTS THE NERDS HAVE
EVER SEEN. SO READ THIS
CAREFULLY, AND YOU MIGHT
JUST LEARN SOMETHING
ABOUT BEING A SPY.

BUT I HAVE MY DOUBTS.

LEVEL 1
ACCESS GRANTED

BEGIN TRANSMISSION:

1

54°46' N, 1°35' W

"How did I get here?" Ruby Peet grumbled to herself as she climbed onto the roof of a British express train. The air was bone-rattling cold, the train was racing at nearly 140 miles an hour, and she was sure the jostling would send her flying over the side at any moment. But, as they say, there isn't any use in complaining when you have a job to do—and Ruby's job was saving the world.

Most people couldn't see past the fact that Ruby was in the sixth grade, only twelve years old, allergic to practically everything in the world, and a social misfit. But the truth was, Pufferfish, as she was known, was actually a very good secret agent.

At that moment, she was in pursuit of a scientist named Dr. Hans Julian, the world's expert on poop. Yes, you read

that correctly. Poop. Dr. Julian knew everything there was to know about dookie, kaka, turds, racing stripes, floaters, and toilet bombs. He also knew how waste could be used for fuels, building materials, and fertilizer, plus a million other very gross things. One could say that he was number one at number two. What he didn't know was how deep the doo-doo would be when he tried to sell some of his knowledge to a very bad person.

What could a guy with a degree in dung know that would put him on the nation's Most Wanted list? Dr. Julian had created a superlaxative that caused intensive, explosive diarrhea. One drop of that liquid in a city's water supply and every man, woman, child, and animal would be racing to the bathroom. With everyone indisposed, any number of crimes could occur and there would be no one to stop them.

She stood, fighting the wind, and peered into the darkness. In the moonlight she spotted Dr. Julian running away from her along the top of the train. Mustering all her courage, she darted after him.

If it were up to her, she'd be calling the shots while one of her fellow agents did the legwork. Gluestick could use his sticky hands and feet to never fall off the train, Braceface could snatch the doctor in a giant fist made from his orthodontic braces, and Wheezer's inhalers would allow her to fly alongside the train and scoop up the bad guy in her arms. Even Flinch's sugar-fueled strength and lightning speed would easily overpower the scientist. Unfortunately, her teammates were on other missions, and Ruby was all by herself. All she had were her allergies—a collection of runny noses, swelling feet, itchy hands, rashes, hives, blisters, and weepy eyes enhanced by the latest science. Coursing through her bloodstream were millions of nanobytes, tiny robots that made her allergic reactions so sensitive she practically had psychic powers. A puffy eye alerted her to explosives. A sudden hacking cough warned her of an assassin's presence. A swollen ankle was a clear sign that she was about to get punched in the face. Her allergies put her one step ahead of every villain, even if she would never know what peanut butter tasted like.

"Dr. Julian! You don't have to do this!" she cried over the howling wind. She wasn't even sure the man could hear her, but it never hurt to use reason before you started using your fists. "You can give me the vial and no one has to get hurt."

Dr. Julian wheeled around, a vial of bright red liquid in his hand. "Kid, you need to leave me alone. You don't know what's going on here."

"I know what you've created, and I know you plan to give it to someone who will use it to take the world hostage. I can't let you do that!"

Dr. Julian snarled and kept running along the top of the

moving train. Ruby raced after him the best she could. At a slight bend in the track, the scientist nearly fell off.

"Dr. Julian!" Ruby cried. If he fell, his vial would fall. The scientists back at the Playground told her that would be disastrous. The superlaxative would seep into the water supply, flow into rivers and oceans, and the world would turn into one big toilet.

Ruby reached the end of her car and took a wild leap, landing hard on the next car. Then she continued to run after the scientist. He had a head start, but she was faster and more

agile, and soon she had cut his lead in half. "You have to stop, Dr. Julian. You know this is wrong."

Julian stopped and faced her. "Kid, my work is for sale to the highest bidder! I can't stop someone from using what I create to do bad things."

Ruby's hands began to swell—a clear sign that Julian was lying. There was more to the scientist's claim. A tickle in her armpit told her that Dr. Julian was being forced against his will.

"Someone has threatened you," Ruby shouted.

"You don't know what you're talking about," he said. "Now get lost before we both get killed."

"What did they say they'd do to you?"

Julian scowled.

Suddenly, Ruby's eyes were swelling, which could only mean one thing: Danger. "Duck!" she shouted with no time to spare. She fell to her belly as the train plunged into a tunnel. She could feel the stone ceiling scraping against her coat, and she prayed that Dr. Julian had been able to heed her warning. When they cleared the tunnel, she got to her feet. The scientist had made it, too.

"Who is making you do this?" she continued.

The words seemed to pain the man. "She's . . . I don't know what her name is, really. She wears a mask with a skull on it."

Ruby felt the air squeeze out of her body. "Ms. Holiday."

"She threatened my family."

"We can protect them," Ruby said, taking a tentative step forward. "I know I look like a meddling kid who is in over her head, but I work with some very powerful people. We can move you and your family to a place she will never find you. You can start over without fear."

Dr. Julian looked down at his vial and then back at her, clearly struggling with the decision. Ruby sympathized and wondered what she would do in the same situation: put her trust in some kid on top of a speeding train, or risk her family's lives?

"All right, kid," he said as he stretched out his arm to hand her the vial.

Ruby let out a deep breath that she hadn't realized she'd been holding. "You're doing the right thing," she said. With her fingertips on the vial, she was suddenly overcome by a tremendous sneezing fit. The vial slipped and fell onto the top of the train. Luckily, it didn't break, but it bounced and skidded toward the far end of the car.

"Hey, Pufferfish, everything OK?" a voice crackled in her head.

Ruby scowled. The sneeze wasn't an allergic reaction or a touch of the flu but what happened when a tiny communication link implanted in Ruby's nose was activated. It was supposed to keep her in close contact with her team members, but as she watched the vial disappear from view, she wished she could reach up her nostril and yank it out. Especially since she knew who was on the other end—Heathcliff Hodges.

"Pufferfish? Can you read me?"

Ruby growled. "You're not supposed to be on the com-link, Heathcliff!"

"I wanted to help. Have you caught Dr. Diarrhea yet? Where are you? It sounds loud—"

Ruby squeezed her nose to deactivate the link and chased after the bouncing vial. It slid across the metal roof, threatening to shatter and explode at any second. She lunged face-first, feeling the slick glass in her hands once more, only to lose it again when another sneeze took hold. Ruby watched the vial hop across the gap to the next car.

"Hey, is everything OK? I think we got disconnected," Heathcliff said over the link. "When you get back, we should run a diagnostic on your nostril implant."

"HEATHCLIFF! If you don't mind, I'm trying to save the world," she said, hauling herself to her feet and disconnecting the com-link. Her eyes again on the vial, she dashed ahead, doing her best to keep her balance with the ever-changing shaking of the train. She was just about to reach down and scoop up the deadly potion again when . . .

"AHHH-CHOOO!"

Her right foot kicked the vial across the gap, sending it onto the next car.

"You have got to be kidding me!" she shouted as her fingers tingled. She was allergic to bad timing and even more sensitive to annoying people.

"Um, I was thinking that maybe I could send a message to the conductor to stop the train. Would that help?"

"I've got it covered!" Ruby bellowed. "And this would be over if you would just leave me alone!"

"Oh," Heathcliff said.

She ignored the hurt in his voice. She knew he was just trying to help, but she didn't have time for him. She squeezed her nose again to shut him out and leaped across the gap. Unfortunately, this landing was not as lucky as the previous ones. Her feet touched down on a patch of black ice that sent her slipping and tumbling over the side of the car. She survived only by snatching a metal railing on the roof with one hand and grabbing the vial out of the air with the other. Strong gusts sent her crashing into the side of the train as she struggled to pull herself back up with one arm. She imagined the bewildered passengers gaping at her through the windows and hoped they would be smart enough to look away before she fell.

Which was exactly what was going to happen. She just didn't have the upper-body strength to hold on for much longer. Death was inevitable, but she had to focus on the vial. When she fell, it would fall, too, which meant it would shatter and soak into the soil.

She refused to be the cause of the world falling apart. There was only one way to stop it. She had to swallow the formula.

She had no idea what the glowing red chemical would do to her body. If a drop could take out a city, what would a whole vial do to her insides? The pain would be staggering, but it would only last a brief moment, and then she would fall and it would all be over. It was the only way to save the world. Dying was part of the deal when she agreed to be a secret agent.

She slipped the little glass tube into her mouth and ground her teeth into the cap in order to yank it off. But she was too late. The train went around a curve, and she was thrown against the car. The force was so strong that her grip was wrenched free and she fell.

But she didn't hit the ground. There was another hand wrapped around her jacket hood, pulling her to safety. She lay on her back, breathing heavily, with the vial still safe—and sealed—between her teeth. In the cold winter air, her savior hovered over her.

"You can't die on me, kid," Dr. Julian said over the wind. "You've got to protect my family."

Ruby nodded and removed the vial from her mouth. She squeezed her nose to reactivate the link to the Playground.

"Heathcliff, are you there? I have something for you to do," she said.

"Really? Oh, boy!" Heathcliff cried.

Ruby set her mouth in a determined expression. "I want Dr. Julian's wife and children taken into protective custody, and I want it done five minutes ago. You tell our people that no one goes home until the Julian family's in a safe house. This is top priority."

Heathcliff squealed with delight. "I'm on it. You can count on me!"

Dr. Julian sat down beside her, lifted the collar on his overcoat, and stared off into the beautiful green fields of northern England, which were slowly becoming more visible in the dawn light.

"So the world owes its continued existence to an eleven-year-old girl?" Dr. Julian asked.

"Actually, I'm twelve," Ruby replied. "And don't worry, Doctor. They only send me when James Bond can't take the job."

"And how often is that?"

Ruby sighed and turned to Dr. Julian. "Lately it's been every day."

2

When you are a supervillain, it is very hard to get respect from the rest of the criminal community if you happen to be cute, and unfortunately, Miss Information was terribly, depressingly adorable. She had big blue eyes, a button nose, tanned skin, and golden hair. She looked like a movie star. Her peers, on the other hand, were covered in ugly scars and had terribly twisted metallic limbs. Some of them had laser eyes or had been disfigured by chemical spills. Professor Zydeco had an alligator head and an accordion frozen in his chest cavity. Miss Information would have loved that! But no luck—she was a beauty. So she was forced to wear a mask that covered her whole head.

The mask had drawbacks.

First, it was very difficult to eat a candy apple while wearing it.

Second, it gave her terrible hat-head.

Third, whenever she called a customer service number and got an automated voice system, it never understood what she was saying. NEVER! She could shout over and over again, but the voice would always say, "I'm sorry. I didn't catch that. Let's try again."

But the mask did have two major pluses. The first was that it scared the living daylights out of everyone who saw it. She'd witnessed people wet their pants or even faint when they met her. That was cool. The second was that she didn't have to look at herself when she wore it. Her face, as lovely as it was, brought on a wave of confusing memories—or were they hallucinations? She couldn't be sure sometimes. It seemed as if she had lived several lives all crammed into one. Was the handsome man with the amazing hair real? Who were the superpowered children that appeared in her dreams? Why did she sometimes ache to wear a cardigan sweater? Why did she have to resist the urge to go into libraries and reshelve books? What was the Dewey decimal system? Why was she always "shushing" people? The mask quieted all of her questions. It made her feel sane.

"I bet they're looking for us, darling," she said. She turned to her boyfriend, who sat in a chair in the corner of her office. He was wearing a tuxedo and holding a white cane, and might have looked very dapper if he wasn't a scarecrow with a head made from a stuffed burlap sack. Miss Information had painted a smiley face on the sack and hung a sign from his neck that read ALEX.

She planted a kiss on the scarecrow's burlap face, then hoisted him over her shoulder. Every step showered loose straw behind her.

She carried Alex into an enormous domed room. The ceiling, which was held aloft by towering pillars, was decorated with intricate ceramic mosaics dedicated to the four branches of evil: raving madmen, world conquerors, firebrand pyromaniacs, and fast-food workers. Below was a room as long and wide as a football field. Hundreds of tables and workstations filled the space, and at each station busy scientists were working feverishly on bizarre inventions: sun-exploding missiles, laser-guided death rays, armies of evil robotic beavers, tidal-wave machines, devices to awaken prehistoric monsters . . . It was like . . . a playground of evil! Every time Miss Information entered the room, she couldn't help but beam with pride. Every detail was built according to her vision—and to think it had all come to her in a dream.

"Miss Information! We've had a breakthrough!"

One of her scientists hobbled across the vast room. She didn't know any of their names, but this one had a ball and chain attached to his leg, which meant he had tried to escape at some point. Miss Information hated when the scientists tried to escape. It really hurt her feelings.

"Oh, yes?" she said. "Which one?"

The scientist removed a folded piece of paper from his pocket and spread it out on a nearby table. It showed a crude drawing of a big circle. Beneath it in neat print were the words *talking*, *flying*, and *robotic ball.*

"Finally!" Miss Information cried. "What took so long?"

The scientist gulped nervously. "We apologize for the delay, but as Dr. Silver remarked, the design was a little vague."

"*Vague?* Everything you needed to know is right here on this paper. Where is this Dr. Silver?"

"You had him placed in a cage full of hungry tigers."

"Oh, *that* Dr. Silver! Well, that'll teach him to be a negative Nelly!"

"Actually, the tigers ate him."

"And now *you're* being a negative Nelly!" she said, huffing. "Why can't you guys be happy? I hired you to work on supercool ideas. This is a dream job for a scientist."

"Um, actually, you kidnapped all of us and force us to work with threats and . . . tigers."

"Listen, I've never run a worldwide criminal enterprise before, so you guys are going to have to cut me some slack! There're going to be some growing pains until I figure it all out. Now, you said you had something to show me?"

He reached into his lab coat and pulled out a silver ball the size of a large tomato. He set it in her hands and pushed a button on its surface. The ball hummed to life. Like magic, it spun like a top and hovered in midair. Purple lights beamed from tiny holes and illuminated the walls and ceiling.

Miss Information turned to her straw boyfriend, who sat in a chair shedding more of his innards onto the floor. "Sweetums! It works."

She turned back to the orb, dazzled by its lights and sounds. "Happy birthday, Benjy!"

A deep, emotionless voice came from within the orb. "Who is Benjy?"

"You are, silly." She giggled. "How do you feel?"

"I do not have hands, so I cannot feel anything."

"No, I don't mean that literally," she replied. "I'm asking about what you are experiencing."

"I do not experience anything. I log and save what I perceive."

Miss Information frowned and turned to the scientist. "I'm unhappy, Mr. Scientisty-man. I thought Benjy would have more sass."

"Sass?"

"You know—personality. I thought he'd be snarky," she said. "This wasn't how I imagined the robot at all. He needs to have opinions and a sense of humor. This thing is totally boring. No offense, Benjy."

"I cannot be offended. I am not programmed with emotions."

"See?" she exclaimed. "Lame!"

"He's a robot, ma'am, with limited artificial intelligence. What you're asking for is simply not possible," the scientist said, his voice shaking.

Miss Information eyed the man disapprovingly. Then she shouted over the din of experiments and chatter, "Does anyone know when the tigers eat lun—"

"But we can fix him!" the scientist cried.

Miss Information turned to her stuffed beau. "Really?" she said as if she were having a conversation. "But I wanted him to be funny. Well, if you think so."

With a pout in her voice she turned back to the scientist. "Let's leave Benjy the way he is." She leaned in to whisper in the terrified man's ear. "I think Alex is a little jealous about the competition for my attention. You should get to work on the next part of my plan."

The scientist nodded and forced a smile on his face. "The machine that gives children superpowers?" he whispered back.

"Yes. You got my designs, correct?"

"I have the crayon drawing of the chair that you drew," he said. "So, yes, I got your designs."

"Well, chop-chop," Miss Information said, raising her voice so everyone could hear. "Time's a-wastin'!"

The scientist darted off as fast as he could with a ball chained to his leg.

"Benjy, welcome to the team. This is Alex, my boyfriend," Miss Information said, gesturing to the straw man. "He's a master spy and an international man of danger."

"That is a scarecrow," Benjy said matter-of-factly.

Miss Information seized the stuffed man and gave him a hug. "Oh, silly, there must be something wrong with your visual sensors."

"My sensors are functioning within—"

"No time for chitchat right now, Benjy. I want to show you our evil headquarters."

Miss Information hoisted the scarecrow onto her back and led the orb through her facility. They passed all manner of space-age vehicles: cars that drove underwater, flying motorcycles, helicopters that ran on maple syrup, mini submarines, and many more. In another room they found weapons: submachine guns, laser pistols, rocket launchers, matter vaporizers—even a flamethrower.

"Look at all my toys, Benjy. We have the most advanced computer and surveillance tech in the world and a full-time staff dedicated to creating one doomsday device after another. And the break room has a juicer! Best of all, we're hidden several stories below a middle school."

Benjy spun around and beeped. "Yes, my internal GPS pinpoints our location as beneath the Margreet Zelle Detention Center for the Incorrigible."

"You are correct. This school houses an army of punks, juvenile delinquents, and bad apples. It's the biggest collection of bullies in North America. They're going to be very helpful in my plans to take over the world."

The orb clicked. "May I ask a question?"

"You betcha."

"Have you given any thought to the logistical complications of maintaining control over the whole world in the highly unlikely event that you succeed? For instance, how will you effectively manage a planet of over seven billion people, all of whom will be plotting to retake their freedom? How will you juggle the various economic needs of each nation? Do you plan on ruling the world with an iron fist or benevolence? Have you found a solution to the needs of poorer countries, or do you plan on subjecting everyone to slavery and destroying the industrialized world? If it is the latter, have you planned for housing, food, clean water, and access to health care? How will you handle the various religious needs of everyone you rule? How do you maintain a single currency for an extremely divergent people who all have different cultural and economic needs?"

Miss Information blinked.

"You haven't thought this out, have you?" the orb asked.

"Never mind all that! Let's get started, shall we?" She stopped at a large screen mounted on the wall and tapped a button on its side. It lit up with the image of a pretty girl no more than twelve years old. She had large mahogany eyes and wore a plaid skirt and a matching sweater with a griffin logo.

"My data bank tells me that this is Tessa Lipton, daughter of the president of the United States," the orb said.

"I know. We're going to kidnap her."

"A second search reveals the criminal penalty for kidnapping the child of a government official is life in prison."

"Oh, don't be a party pooper, Benjy," Miss Information said. "This is going to be superfun!"

3

38°51' N, 77°4' W

To avoid confusion, Ruby had created a chart to ensure that she was never late for school.

6:45 WAKE UP, TURN OFF ALARM CLOCK

6:50 TAKE ALLERGY MEDICINE

6:55 SHOWER

7:05 TOWEL-DRY/ATTEMPT TO DETANGLE KINKY HAIR

7:10 CHECK TIME TO MAKE SURE SCHEDULE IS WORKING

7:15 GIVE UP ON KINKY HAIR, GET DRESSED

7:25 SAY GOOD MORNING TO PARENTS (NOTE: FRANCIS AND SARAH) AND BABY BROTHER (NOAH)

7:27 PET THE DOG (TRUMAN) THEN LET HIM OUT THE BACK DOOR TO DO HIS "BUSINESS"

7:28 PARTICIPATE IN LIGHT CHITCHAT/BONDING WITH FAMILY

7:35 EAT BREAKFAST

7:50 DOUBLE CHECK TIME TO INSURE SCHEDULE IS BEING MAINTAINED

7:55 FLOSS AND BRUSH

8:00 MAKE SECOND ATTEMPT AT DETANGLING HAIR

8:10 SURRENDER TO FUTILITY OF KINKY HAIR, GATHER BELONGINGS

8:15 PUT ON COAT, BOOTS, HAT, MITTENS, AND SCARF (WINTER SCHEDULE)

8:20 MORE CHITCHAT WITH FAMILY; GOOD-BYE HUGS AND KISSES

8:30 DEPART FOR SCHOOL

Unfortunately, her family had a way of smashing her plans with a wrecking ball and then setting them on fire. At 6:55, when she should have been showering, she heard a calamity in the kitchen she could not ignore. Grumbling, she padded through the house and found Sarah burning scrambled eggs while talking on the phone. Francis was attempting to spoon-feed Noah while trying to knot his necktie with his free hand, and Truman, the family terrier, was throwing himself against the back door with a panicked whine.

Ruby sighed and took charge. She let the dog out. Then she turned and took the frying pan from Sarah, replacing it with a container of orange juice, and spinning her toward the glasses already on the table. The eggs were a lost cause—crunchy and black—so Ruby tossed them in the garbage and cracked a half-dozen fresh eggs into a bowl. She lowered the flame on the stove and beat the eggs with a whisk. After pouring them in a frying pan, she stuffed four slices of bread into the toaster with one hand while rinsing a bunch of grapes with the other.

She snatched a roll of paper towels off the counter and went to work cleaning the baby food off Noah and everything else within five yards of him. Ruby took the tie from her father, wrapped it around her own neck, and tied it for him. Then she went back to the eggs for a quick stir, tossed some cheese on them, gave them a flip, and served them onto three plates. When the glasses were full of juice, Ruby guided her mother to her seat, then gave her a butter knife and pointed her toward a fresh stack of toast while she poured coffee into both of her parents' oversize mugs.

"Did you get any sleep last night?" her father asked her while attempting to insert a spoon full of creamed rice into Noah's mouth. The little boy's lips were clamped shut like a vise.

"Just a little tired," Ruby said. The truth was she was exhausted and felt like she was shuffling around like a zombie. After her mission on the train, she felt that she needed at least a week of solid sleep to recover, but she couldn't tell her parents about it. Though she felt icky lying to them, she truly believed that keeping them in the dark also kept them safe. "Try the choo-choo trick."

Francis smiled. "What would we do without you, Ruby?"

"You'd be up to your ears in dirty diapers and the house would be on fire," Ruby said.

Just then, she let out a terrible sneeze.

"Honey, did you take your allergy medicine?" Sarah asked.

"I'll take care of it right now," Ruby said, excusing herself from the table and rushing to the bathroom. She locked the door and squeezed her nose. "Pufferfish here."

The principal sounded agitated. "Kid, I need you and the team here pronto. We've got a national emergency."

"What's new? I suppose it's another insane plot by Ms. Holiday?"

There was an uncomfortable silence on the other end. No one liked to think their biggest enemy had once been one of their best friends.

"Just hurry, and if you happen to have a pleated skirt, bring it with you."

"A pleated skirt?"

The com-link disconnected.

The principal sounded panicked. Tired as she was, she knew she had to put her morning into high gear. She opened the bathroom door, prepared to race to her room to get dressed, but she was stopped by her mother waiting on the other side.

"I need you home on time tonight, Ruby. No excuses,"

Sarah said. "The entire family is coming in two days for our annual Hanukkah and Christmas celebration. Grandma Rose and Grandpa Tom, Grandma Tina and Grandpa Saul, Aunt Delynn, Aunt Denise, Aunt Suzi, Aunt Laura, Aunt Emily, Uncle JJ, Uncle Justin, Uncle Eddie, Uncle Kevin, Uncle Jeff, Uncle Christopher, Uncle John, and all your cousins—Kiah, Kiara, Leaf, Finn, Hayley, Tulia, Siena, Danny, Alex, Charlotte, Kate, and Imogen. We have to get ready."

Ruby groaned. "All seven thousand of them? They aren't staying here, are they?"

"Sure, because I'm trying to blow up the house," her mother said with a laugh. "You know we can't keep all the Protestants and Jews in the same house for longer than an hour before a holy war starts. Don't worry—your father booked them into a hotel. But we're hosting a couple big dinners here and I want this place spick-and-span. I could also use some of your famous organizing skills."

"You're trying to distract me from this insane inconvenience with my love of making lists," Ruby grumbled.

Sarah smiled. "If you want to be in this family, you have to have an appetite for chaos. Come home right after school."

"Fine, but I have some rules. The little ones have to stay out of my room. They're like ferrets going through my drawers, pulling things out, and dragging them all over the house," Ruby said. "I have a system."

"OK."

"And I absolutely insist that everyone read the visitors handbook I made for the house, especially the part about how to use the remote control for the television. Remember last year, when Grandpa Saul got his hands on it? Pandemonium."

"Deal!" Sarah said, throwing her arms around her daughter and hugging her tight.

"Mom! Hugging is supposed to happen at 8:20. You're messing up the schedule!"

END TRANSMISSION.

TOP SECRET DOSSIER
CODE NAME: BIGFOOT
REAL NAME: PEGGY GRUNT
YEARS ACTIVE: 1994-99
CURRENT OCCUPATION:
FOREST RANGER

HISTORY: PEGGY'S AWKWARD STAGE, FROM THE AGE OF TEN UNTIL FOURTEEN, WAS ONE OF THE WORLD'S MOST DISTURBING. SHE HAD ARMS THAT HUNG NEARLY TO HER FEET AND AN UNFORTUNATE UNDERBITE THAT RENDERED MUCH OF WHAT SHE SAID UNINTELLIGIBLE. SHE CAME TO THE TEAM'S ATTENTION AFTER SHE WAS CAPTURED BY HUNTERS WHILE ON A SCHOOL FIELD TRIP TO COLLECT LEAVES. WHEN THE HUNTERS TRIED TO SELL HER TO A CIRCUS, NERDS RESCUED HER AND OFFERED HER A PLACE ON THE TEAM. SHE WAS A FAITHFUL SPY UNTIL SHE TURNED FIFTEEN AND SUDDENLY WENT FROM UGLY DUCKLING TO SUPERHOT BABE.

UPGRADE: BIGFOOT PRODUCED A
PHEROMONE THAT CAUSED BOYS TO
FALL IN LOVE WITH HER, MAKING
THEM HIGHLY SUGGESTIBLE TO
HER REQUESTS.

LEVEL 2
ACCESS GRANTED

BEGIN TRANSMISSION:

4

38°52' N, 77°6' W

The team assembled at the mission desk in the Playground and waited for the principal to arrive. Heathcliff hunkered in the shadows. He knew he was forbidden from taking part in mission briefings, but he just couldn't help himself. Being a spy was exciting, and it frustrated him that he wasn't allowed to help. Plus, he wanted to be ready for the day when they invited him back on the team.

"Another mission?" Matilda cried. "This is ridiculous!"

"If Ms. Holiday is behind this one, I'm going to scream," Duncan said. "We just stopped her from melting the polar ice caps last week!"

"Don't forget the man-eating plants that attacked Birmingham," Jackson added.

"And when she poisoned the world's supply of corn dogs," Flinch grumbled.

"The earthquake machine was no day in the park, either!" Duncan said.

"They know we're only twelve years old, right?" Jackson roared.

Heathcliff understood their frustration. The team had been working eighteen-hour days for months, keeping the world from exploding or falling into chaos. They were understaffed and underappreciated.

Ruby stood up and raised a hand to calm everyone. She was a natural-born leader and the team's spokesperson. Heathcliff and Ruby had knocked heads many times when he was on the team, but he always respected her.

"I'll handle this," she said. "The principal will understand. I think that a few staff additions will make a huge difference. We need a gadget tech to teach us the latest stuff coming out of the science team. We need a surveillance expert to go over what's happening around the world. We need an information specialist and a historian—"

"—and a new Benjamin!" Duncan said.

Ruby nodded. "Yes, a new Benjamin would be helpful, plus a pilot for the School Bus now that the lunch lady is the principal. I don't feel comfortable flying around in a remote-control rocket."

"Um, hello?" Jackson said, raising his hand. "I'd be happy to train for that job. I have excellent eye-hand coordination and I look hot in aviator sunglasses."

"We can't have a child flying a supersonic jet," Matilda said.

"Oh, but we can have one jumping out of it to fight robots and mad scientists?"

Just then, the principal walked into the room, and the team turned their anger on him. The five of them were like a pack of angry dogs, yipping and barking at the bewildered man.

"What in the world is wrong with you people?" the principal asked.

"We're tired!"

"We're overworked!"

"We're frustrated!"

"We haven't been in a classroom in months!"

"The snack machine is out of taffy!"

Everyone looked at Flinch.

"Well, it is," he said defensively.

Heathcliff knew it was time to act. "Maybe I can help," he said as he stepped into the light.

The principal frowned. "Listen, Heathcliff, we're having a team meeting and—"

"Just hear me out, OK?" No one argued, so he continued. "I know how to fix this team. You're outmatched. Ms. Holiday is springing one world-ending scheme after another on you. Some days you even have to split up, which weakens the team. That's not how this group is supposed to work. The team is falling apart."

"Duh!" Matilda said. "Tell us something we don't know."

This was more than Matilda had said to him in weeks, and Heathcliff faultered. They thought he was criticizing them. He had to find the right words to win them over.

"You guys are the best of the best," he said. "I believe Ms. Holiday is intentionally trying to wear you out. Her schemes are outlandish and impractical. You've stopped most of them without much effort. They're not supposed to be hard. They're supposed to be frequent."

"No one would know better about end-of-the-world scheming than you," Jackson said with a chuckle. The others gave him an angry look and he blushed.

Despite Heathcliff's ravenous hunger for information about his past, he brushed the clue aside. He had to stay focused on his goal. "What I'm saying is, you could use some help, and I think I can be that help. I want back on the team."

An uncomfortable silence filled the room. It was not the response Heathcliff was hoping for, but he wasn't giving up.

"You wouldn't have to train me. I remember all the fighting styles, the code-breaking, even how to free-fall from the School

Bus. All you would need to do is put me in the upgrade chair and—"

The principal shook his head. "Heathcliff, you *are* helping—by manning the communication link."

Heathcliff frowned. "You could have a monkey do that job. You need another agent. I'm smart and have tons of experience."

His former friends didn't have to say no to him. Their faces shouted it from across the room. Why were they so resistant to letting him help? It had to do with the missing year and a half of his life, but what was it?

"I don't get it. You let *Jackson Jones* onto the team. He's got to be the worst person in the world. No offense."

"None taken," Jackson said.

"What could I have done that would be worse than the torment he's been dishing out since kindergarten?"

"For the record, I think I've changed," Jackson mumbled.

"Heathcliff, this isn't the time for this," Ruby said. "When things have settled down a little, maybe we can talk—"

"—and until then I'm a prisoner—"

"You are not a prisoner," the principal interrupted.

"Really? Then I can go home?" he asked, knowing full well the answer would be no.

"Heathcliff, I've explained this to you before," the principal said. "We had to erase your parents' memory of you."

"But you haven't told me why!"

He watched Ruby wrestle with an explanation.

"No one thought you were going to come back," Matilda said.

"Where did I go?" Heathcliff shouted. He could hear the echo of his anger bounce around the room.

"We're working on a way to reverse the memory wipe," the principal said. "Until then, you just have to be patient. What we're trying to do to your mom and dad has never been done before, and we get only one chance. I assure you it will happen soon, but right now you have to stay here. If you need more books or magazines to keep you occupied, I can—"

Heathcliff threw up his hands. "Books and magazines? No. You know what I need? Some friends!"

He stomped out of the room, desperate to get back to his little cot before he started crying. He felt so useless, so hated, so homesick, and so alone.

5

38°53' N, 77°5' W

"Sugarland Academy," Ruby said as she and her teammates stood at the entrance to one of the country's most elite private schools, tucked away on fifty acres in Arlington, Virginia. With high, sweeping glass walls, an observatory, an Olympic-size swimming pool, tennis courts, and a private golf course, it provided every possible opportunity for its students. While the rest of the team complained about the school's starchy uniforms, Ruby grew more and more envious the more she learned about it. A year's tuition at Sugarland was almost the same as a semester at Harvard Law School, but the staff was made up of elected officials, former CEOs, and world-renowned scholars. It was also founded by the man who invented the personal organizer. The school's motto was "An organized mind is the

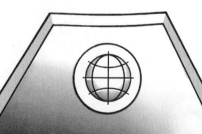

seed of success." Ruby thought she had died and gone to heaven.

"Why make a school this fancy?" Jackson said, eyeing the building warily. "If the kids who go here are anything like they are at our school, they'll just cover it in spit wads."

Ruby shook her head. "These kids aren't like the baboons we go to school with, Jackson. They pride themselves on being serious. They grow up to run everything."

"You sound like you'd like to be one of them," Duncan said as he yanked at his uniform collar.

"I'd never make it here if I had to wear this getup all the time," Matilda said, struggling with her skirt. "Reminds me of going undercover as a cheerleader. I never want to wear a skirt again."

"It's prestigious."

"It's itchy."

"But look, Matilda. There's a scary griffin sewn onto the sweater," Jackson said, pointing at the school's crest in burgundy and gold. "It looks like it wants to murder something and then eat it."

"*Grragggh!*" Flinch said, aping a scary monster. The rest of the team laughed.

Ruby scowled.

"I assume everyone saw the Secret Service agents," the principal said.

"There are a few on the roof, and I saw one in a tree,"

38°53' N, 77°5' E

Jackson said. "What I wouldn't give for a carton of eggs right now. There's nothing so fun as tossing eggs at someone who has climbed up a tree."

"Yeah, I remember you doing that to me. I just don't remember it being fun," Duncan said, rolling his eyes.

"Does everyone know their cover stories? Jackson, your father owns the Cleveland Browns. Duncan, your mother made a fortune on an Internet startup where people could purchase their groceries online. Matilda, your mom is the CEO of Suckerpunch Mixed Martial Arts, Inc., and Flinch, your dad invented Raisinets."

"Don't I wish!" Flinch cried.

"Pufferfish, you're the heir to a squirtable-cheese empire."

"Huh?"

"Your mission is to protect Tessa Lipton," the principal said, ignoring Ruby's confused expression. "Oh, and keep your upgrades off-line."

"What? No powers?" Matilda cried.

"Not unless you want one of those government workers to go back to the office and tell their bosses that a bunch of kids with superpowers helped keep the president's daughter safe."

Once inside, Ruby marveled at the floors, which were waxed to a mirror shine. Photographs of famous Sugarland Academy alumni decorated the walls, many of whom Ruby recognized from the world of politics. Two of them were former presidents. But it was the students who truly impressed her. They walked to their classes in single-file lines, spoke in hushed tones, and behaved like grown-ups. Not one of them had drawn a mustache or a goatee on any of the portraits. There was no goofing off, no pulling pranks, and no shoving people into lockers. Ruby felt like Dorothy Gale, swept away by a twister and dropped into a magical world, except, unlike Dorothy, Ruby didn't want to go home.

She couldn't help but feel that this was where she was supposed to be. Sure, she loved her friends, but sometimes she wondered if being a spy was really all it was cracked up to be. Her life was so chaotic, every day a new disaster. Even when they did beat the bad guys, ten more popped up to take their place. Plus, she was missing a lot of classes in order to save the world, and she worried about the long-term effects of going to school without really going to school. Once she turned sixteen, the team would cut her loose to fend for herself, but if she went to *this* school, the bastion of intellect and planning, she would be prepared for a life of power and prestige. Maybe she should transfer. Sure, she would have to give up her upgrades, but she'd get to go to a school that taught a class on "the art of sitting still"! She wasn't sure if a person could have a school for a soul mate, but she was certain she was falling in love with Sugarland Academy.

38°53' N, 77°5' E

The principal escorted them to the main office, where they met Ms. Turnston, the school secretary. Turnston was a bony woman who couldn't have weighed more than the paperweight on her desk. Her serious, tight-faced expression seemed to suggest that laughter was something that should be eliminated for the safety of others. Oddly enough, Ruby found the woman's lack of humor comforting. It was nice to be around people who took life seriously.

"Are these the five new students I was informed would be arriving today?" Ms. Turnston asked sourly.

The principal leaned in close. "Yes, and I hope you'll use your discretion. These children have very important families."

The secretary's frown deepened. "Sugarland's student body is made up of the upper echelon of the elite of Washington, D.C.," she snapped. "Discretion is this school's top priority."

Her sermon made the principal take a step back. "Very good," he said, nodding.

The NERDS were required to read and sign several codes of conduct. One strictly prohibited silliness, and another threatened expulsion for "the passing of gas, the picking of boogers, or the digging for earwax." Ruby saw her friends bristle at all the rules, but she secretly loved them, especially the pamphlet on the proper steps for asking a question.

The principal and the children took a brief tour of the

grounds, including the school's greenhouse, film production studio, art museum, and rock climbing wall, then Ms. Turnston gave them their class schedules and a farewell scowl. "I trust you can find your way from here, and, please, stay off the grass. It's imported from Iceland."

"Wow, even the grass is fancy," Jackson said.

"Remember, no upgrades," the principal said after wishing them luck. "Don't let Tessa out of your sight, and stay in touch."

He slipped away, leaving the children alone.

"We should probably not hang out together," Ruby told the others. "People will notice that the five new kids are suddenly best friends."

Matilda nodded. "Makes sense."

"I'll keep an eye on the cafeteria. I hear they have a pastry chef on staff!" Flinch said, licking his lips.

"And I've got the outside of the school covered," Duncan said, removing a remote control from his backpack. He flipped a switch and a dozen floating pods materialized in the air. "I brought the Hovercraft Robotic Surveillance L-114a's."

"Um, the what?" Jackson said.

"Don't you guys have any interest in the gadgets our science team creates for us?" Duncan said, sighing. "These are floating cameras with a space-age camouflage mode that makes them invisible to the naked eye. They're whisper-quiet, too."

He pushed a button and the machines vanished as quickly as they appeared.

"I have them positioned all over the campus," Duncan continued. "If Ms. Holiday shows up, we'll see her coming a mile away."

"Smart thinking, Gluestick," Ruby said. "All right, let's keep our real eyes on Tessa, and remember, she's a person surrounded by dignitaries and royalty. If you must talk to her—and I highly recommend that you don't—but if you do, try not to act like morons and idiots."

Her teammates stared back at her, offended. Then they scowled and walked away, leaving Ruby all alone.

"Not that you act like morons and idiots . . . all the time. Just some of the time!" she called after them.

Ruby stalked Tessa Lipton. She followed her down hallways and into bathrooms, and hovered while Tessa drank from the water fountain. It wasn't long before Ruby had a pretty clear picture of who the first daughter was: the queen of Sugarland Academy. Tessa held every student in the palm of her hand. Kids raced to get her lunch. They rubbed her tired feet. They carried her books to class. One even offered to chew her food. At first Ruby chalked up Tessa's popularity to her being the daughter of the most famous person in the United States, but when she was told the son of the country's most famous actor and the daughter of the world's biggest-selling hip-hop artist also went to Sugarland, she realized that was too simple of an explanation.

There had to be another reason, and Ruby was determined to discover it. She decided to do recon at lunch, so she invited herself to eat with a trio of girls whose table had the best view of Tessa's "permanent" seat. Their names were Deonne, Charlotte, and Mary Alice, and as luck would have it they were the best of friends, notorious gossips, and overly impressed by wealth and fame.

"You're the daughter of Harvey Pickens—the squirtable-cheese billionaire? Wow! You are so lucky. At my house, our servants are forced to slice the cheese by hand!" Deonne said. She was as thin as a flagpole, with a set of braces that even Jackson would find unsettling.

"My father says it is unbecoming to feel sympathy for the help," Charlotte whispered. She wore sunglasses and said everything in a hushed tone.

"Oh, Charlotte. We're not barbarians," Mary Alice said. She had long, luxurious red hair and more freckles on her face than there were stars in the sky. "If cheese can be squirted, the servants are wasting valuable time best spent running our baths and attending to our ponies."

"I guess you are right," Charlotte said.

"So, I hear the president's daughter goes here," Ruby said.

"Oh, yes," Deonne replied. "Tessa. Quite a lovely girl."

"Lovely," Charlotte peeped.

"A true gem," Mary Alice added.

Ruby was suddenly envious. "So you're friends with her?"

"Oh, no," Mary Alice said. "She's horrible."

"Horrid, really," Deonne agreed.

"Foul," Charlotte said, then looked around to make sure she was not heard.

"I'm confused," Ruby said. "I thought you said she was lovely."

"To look at," Charlotte whispered. "But her personality is awful."

"She's mean! And rude!" Mary Alice added.

"She's what my yacht captain would call 'insufferable,'" Deonne said. "But you didn't hear that from us."

"She has a lot of power at this school," Mary Alice said.

"You don't want to cross her. Last year she was so mean, a girl fled the country and sought asylum in Iraq," Charlotte whispered.

When Ruby ran into Flinch in the hallway, his face was covered in blueberry pie.

"THIS SCHOOL HAS A BAKERY!" he shouted, barely able to control his shaking body.

"I *told* you it was a special place," she said. "But you need to stop eating sweets. You're going to freak out, and besides, you have pie all over you."

"I didn't eat this pie. Tessa Lipton shoved my face in it. She's vicious. She stomped on my lunch. Twenty-five oatmeal cream cookies died an early death because of her. What am I supposed to eat for my fifth desert today? I didn't bring a backup treat!"

"I'm sorry about your cookies. Just keep your distance. Be subtle."

Flinch beat on his chest and bellowed. "I am the KING OF SUBTLETY!"

Later, Jackson was waiting for Ruby after her class on the History of Quiet Amusements. They found seats in the back of the library and spoke in whispers.

"If Ms. Holiday needed an inside man to help her kidnap Tessa, she wouldn't lack for volunteers. All the students hate her guts," he said. "Most of the teachers, too. Apparently, little Ms. Lipton runs this place like a dictator, only with a lot less mercy. The last principal quit because Tessa kept sending her mean texts."

"I know, Flinch told me," Ruby said gloomily.

"You're disappointed with her?"

"No, I'm disappointed with the school. I thought it was different."

"Sorry, Puff. Every school has a bully, even a school with a space shuttle and a hospital attached to it. You don't belong here, anyway."

Ruby blushed. It was as if Jackson had read her dreamy thoughts about being a Sugarland griffin.

"Everyone here is too bossy," he continued. "Who would you tell what to do?"

Pufferfish growled, but Jackson just laughed. "Do you think that maybe we've got this one wrong?" he asked. "Kidnapping isn't Ms. Holiday's style. Most of her stunts are giant robots and mutant bunnies."

"I don't think we know anything about her anymore. When she clobbered Agent Brand and tried to kill Flinch, I chalked it up to her being infected by the villain virus. But when we destroyed the corrupted nanobytes, she was still evil and crazy. She's obsessed with taking over the world, and kidnapping the president's daughter is probably a good way to do it. President Lipton would hand over anything to save his kid."

Jackson sighed. "Ms. Holiday was the coolest adult I knew. I'm sure you guys would have kicked me off the team if not for her."

"We *did* kick you off the team," Ruby reminded him.

"Yes, but luckily I am charming and friendly and a valuable asset," Jackson replied.

Just then, Matilda stormed in, receiving a big shush from the librarian. Wheezer ignored her and approached her teammates.

"The president's daughter called me a pigface," she said. "I'm going to kill her and before you tell me no, let me remind you that our mission is to keep her from being kidnapped. Technically, we succeed if she's dead."

"You can't kill her," Ruby said.

"What if I put her in the hospital? Nothing serious—just a broken face."

All three agents sneezed simultaneously. Gluestick was on the com-link. "If Tessa gets kidnapped, how bad would it be if we didn't try to rescue her?"

"You had a run-in with her, too?" Ruby asked.

"Yes, and so did my underpants. I'm going to be pulling them out of my behind until I'm old and gray. Her forearms have monkey strength!"

"Listen, team, this isn't the first time we've had to protect someone who was intolerable," Ruby said.

"Yeah, but Tessa isn't a swimsuit model like the last one," Jackson grumbled.

"Luckily, Tessa is probably safe," Duncan said. "The day is almost over and we haven't had as much as a whisper from Miss Information."

Jackson nodded. "We should call the principal and let him know we're going to be following the First Jerk around again tomorrow."

Suddenly, Ruby felt the floor begin to shake. She held on to her seat and watched as several books fell off the shelves and tumbled to the floor. "Duncan, what's going on?" She asked. "Are there tanks outside?"

"There's nothing outside," Duncan said. "I have no idea where that noise is coming from."

The sound was getting louder and the shaking more intense. "What about a helicopter?" Jackson asked.

"What kind of helicopter cracks marble floors?" Matilda asked.

"The walls in the main office are crumbling like crackers," Duncan said.

Pufferfish, Braceface, and Wheezer ran out of the library and toward the noise. In the hallway there was an explosion of snapping wood, pulverized concrete, bursting pipes, and boiling steam.

"Maybe it's an earthquake!" Flinch cried as he joined the com-link.

Ruby shook her head. "It's not an earthquake. It's her, and she's not coming from the sky or outside. She's coming from underneath! Where is Tessa right now?"

"She's in pre-algebra," Duncan shouted. "Room 111-A."

"Go!" Ruby shouted, and she, Jackson, and Matilda dashed off to find the classroom. As they turned the corner, Flinch appeared like a lightning flash in a thunderstorm. The hall was empty so no one spotted his superspeed. Duncan joined them outside of Tessa's class, but it was too late. They could see through the window in the classroom door that the floor was buckling, being thrust upward as a large, metallic drill broke the surface.

Ruby threw open the door. "Everyone listen up. Get out of this room now!" she shouted, but the students were far too shocked and terrified to follow instructions. "Listen to me! All of you are in danger. I need everyone to get up from their desks and—"

She didn't get to finish. The drill shot up out of the floor like a whale breaching the waves. It fell down hard on its side, knocking students and desks over in a massive shock wave.

The agents leaped into action when the large machine fired a rocket directly at them, a plume of black smoky death trailing behind it. Ruby barely had time to shout a warning and dive out of the way before the missile crashed into the very spot where she and the NERDS had been standing. Ruby staggered to her feet and squinted through the black air for Tessa Lipton. She couldn't let Ms. Holi—no, Miss Information—take the president's daughter, but she couldn't see and her ears were buzzing like they had been colonized by honeybees.

But Ruby "Pufferfish" Peet didn't need any of those senses. She had a sixth sense her doctor called "overactive allergies." She closed her eyes and tried to tune out the screech in her ears. Instead, she listened to the messages her body was telling her. Her puffy glands and runny nose were speaking loud and clear.

A row of red sores appeared on her forearm. She knew what that meant—goons. She was allergic to goons, and by the number of bumps she could tell there were eight of them spilling out of a hatch in the machine. A sudden swelling in her right big toe meant one was in striking distance. She swung, made contact, and felt the bad guy slump to the floor. Now there were seven bumps, so only seven goons. But where were they? The itching of her ear allowed her to play a game of hotter/colder. The closer she got to the next villain, the more her ear itched, and soon she was whacking him in the jaw. Six bumps.

A phlegmy cough meant there was someone behind her. She was allergic to being snuck up on. A quick turn matched with a swift kick to the goon's groin sent him toppling over in pain. Wait—puffy lips! A fast elbow behind her, right into the Adam's apple of another of Miss Information's toadies. Four bumps left.

"Pufferfish, are you OK?" Duncan shouted through the noise. "We can't see you!"

"I'm fine," Ruby said, smashing another goon in the face. "Find Tessa!"

But then there was a ridge of red, hot sores sprouting up her back. She was allergic to betrayal. The only explanation: Miss Information had arrived.

"I can't let you do this, Ms. Holiday," Ruby cried, forgetting her old friend's alias in the panic of the moment.

"Don't call me that!" the former librarian bellowed. "My name is Miss Information—or Master, if you want to get a head start on what the world will soon be calling me."

Even through the mask Ruby could hear the woman's rage. Why did she hate to be called by her real name? Was she really that disconnected from reality? If only Ruby could reach her, take her by the hand, and let her know they still loved her. Unfortunately, she had more immediate problems. A stinging pain in her ears told her that the other goons had surrounded her. She was allergic to being surrounded.

She swung at one, clipping him in the temple, and he fell over with a thud. Her right leg shot out behind her and nailed a second thug in the belly. She could hear the wind exploding out of his mouth even if she couldn't see his face through the smoke. There was only one punk left to worry about and then she could deal with Ms. Holiday, but he had abandoned the fight and snatched Tessa. He dragged the poor, screaming girl into the bizarre drill machine while Miss Information looked on.

"Don't do this, Ms. Holiday!" Ruby begged.

The villain stood motionless, staring at Ruby. She tilted her head as if trying to shake something loose from her brain. For a moment, Ruby believed she had gotten through to the former librarian. But then another rocket fired out of the machine, and Ruby was forced to leap for her life once more. By the time she had recovered, the drill was spinning and the machine was slipping back into the massive sinkhole. There was nothing Ruby or anyone else could do to stop it.

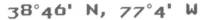

6

Even though Miss Information had technically kidnapped Tessa, she still wanted to make a good impression. So when her goons brought the frightened, tired girl to meet her, she had a plate of freshly baked chocolate chip cookies ready.

"Have a cookie, sweetie. I made them myself," she said.

Tessa eyed the treats suspiciously. "You're in big trouble, lady! My father won't rest until I'm found. He'll send the military, the Secret Service, the CIA, and the FBI. If he has to, he'll even send the Boy Scouts!"

"Oh, honey, you know that's not true. Your daddy is far too concerned with his next election to make a big scene out of getting you back. How would it look to voters if he can't protect his own daughter? No, I think what will most likely

happen is, he'll quietly do everything to find you, and then he'll attempt to negotiate your return at a bargain price. He likes being president, and he's not about to let you ruin it for him."

Miss Information watched Tessa's face fall. She got no pleasure in hurting the girl's feelings, but young Ms. Lipton needed to see the truth if she was going to be of any use.

"I know how it must feel," Ms. Holiday continued. "You're not his top priority, and that's heartbreaking. But he does have a long history of disappointing you, doesn't he? When he was the mayor of Arlington, he missed your preschool graduation. When he was the governor of Virginia, he went to a campaign fund-raiser lunch instead of your ballet recital. He was a no-show at your soccer team's championship and even a couple of Christmases. You're a very forgiving person to let him get away with it, Tessa. You're a much stronger person than me."

"You don't understand. His job isn't easy," Tessa snapped.

"That's what your mother says to make you feel better, right? I'm sure she's very worried about you, but she'll keep quiet. She's really not a wave-maker, is she? So sad. You're just not on their list of priorities."

"How do you know that?" Tessa whispered.

"I know lots of things, Tessa. After all, they do call me Miss Information. For instance, I know that your kidnapping has been completely covered up."

"Impossible! All my friends saw you take me!"

Miss Information snatched a remote control off a nearby table and aimed it at a wall of television screens. Every major news channel was broadcasting live. Not one of them was talking about Tessa.

"That's kind of odd, don't you think? The president's daughter is taken against her will in front of her classmates and there's not a peep on the news? What's on CNN? Oh, a report about a squirrel that water-skis. Well, that's huge international news, right? Watch this—he's going to jump a ramp. Wow, that animal is fearless."

Tears began to well in Tessa's eyes. Miss Information's plan was working perfectly. Now it was time to be a friend. She got up from her chair and wrapped an arm around the girl's shoulders. "Now, now, there's no need to cry."

Tessa pulled away from her angrily. "He'll come for me and you're going to go to jail forever."

Miss Information frowned. "I guess we're going to find out, Tessa. In the meantime, you look like you could use some rest. Guards, take Ms. Lipton to her room—not the cell. Run a hot bath for her and then send in the massage therapist and the manicurist. Also, find out if there is anything she would like to eat. Ms. Lipton is our guest."

"So I'm not a hostage?"

"No, you're still a hostage. Did I say 'guest'? I meant . . . well . . . what's a nicer word than *prisoner*? *Captive*? *Detainee*? Oh, it doesn't matter. Honey, the point is: Get comfortable. We're going to be here awhile."

TOP SECRET DOSSIER

CODE NAME: BELL BOTTOM
REAL NAME: JEAN GREENE
YEARS ACTIVE: 1979-84
CURRENT OCCUPATION:
FASHION DESIGNER

HISTORY: JEAN GREENE WAS
BROUGHT IN TO REPLACE AGENT
GHOST WHEN GHOST LEFT THE
TEAM AFTER HER PARENTS
DISCOVERED HER SPY ACTIVITIES.
JEAN'S EARLY LIFE WAS
TUMULTUOUS. SHE WAS KNOWN FOR
STEALING CARS AND GOING ON
JOYRIDES—PRIMARILY IN
TRANS AMS. THE PROBLEM WAS,
SHE WAS ELEVEN YEARS OLD.

UPGRADE: PRE-NANOBYTE
TECHNOLOGY. JEAN'S GIGANTIC
FLARING PANTS WERE EQUIPPED
WITH HUNDREDS OF TOOLS AND
WEAPONS SHE COULD ACCESS JUST
BY SHAKING HER LEG.

LEVEL 3
ACCESS GRANTED

BEGIN TRANSMISSION:

7

38°52' N, 77°6' W

Heathcliff got no pleasure from being right, so when the team returned from Sugarland Academy, he didn't meet them. It didn't seem appropriate to rub salt in their wounds, especially since the principal was busy doing that himself.

"It's time to accept reality. You need help. I'm recruiting new members immediately."

"Agreed!" Duncan cried.

"Forget new members. Just put Heathcliff in the upgrade chair and let him back on the team," Jackson said.

Heathcliff was stunned. Of all the people in the world, he never expected Jackson to be on his side.

"Agreed," Duncan said again.

"No way," Matilda said, though it sounded like she was yawning. "Not after what he's done."

"Agreed," Duncan said.

"Huh?"

"Sorry," Duncan said. "I'm just so tired, I'm having trouble keeping track of this conversation."

"Put your head back on the table, Duncan," Jackson said.

"Thank you."

"*Graagggghhhh,*" Flinch said. "What if 'nice-guy Heathcliff' goes back to being 'bad-guy Heathcliff' after we've given him upgrades? I vote no."

"We're not voting," Ruby said. "We don't need someone unstable on the team."

Bad-guy Heathcliff? Unstable? Heathcliff felt his heart break.

"We have to do *something*, Pufferfish," the principal said.

"Who's going to train these new recruits? And what happens if they wash out? Then we have to wipe their minds of all they've learned about us. The kids who can't hack it are never the same. Most of them walk through the halls with crayons shoved up their noses, claiming to be Teenage Mutant Ninja Turtles. Remember Bobby Rickle? He thinks he's an electric eel. He runs up and pinches people on the butt."

"The Shocker?" Jackson says. "You guys did that to him? That's hilarious."

"No, it's sad!" Ruby replied.

"And sad," Jackson echoed, breaking into a giggling fit.

"Then I'll bring in the Troublemakers," the principal said. "You've all worked with the Hyena, and Flinch has a good relationship with the others."

Ruby banged the table. "Those guys don't fix problems; they make them. Absolutely not."

"Ruby, be reasonable," Duncan said.

"Nope. No way. No Troublemakers. No new members I can't control. No Heathcliff and his unstable brain. If you add anyone to this team, I will quit. We can handle this ourselves."

Heathcliff crept back to his room and lay down on his cot.

Unstable.

What did that mean? He didn't feel unstable. He felt like a normal twelve-year-old boy—albeit a very smart twelve-year-old boy. If he were unstable, wouldn't he have symptoms? Wouldn't he be yammering to himself about conspiracies and wearing a tinfoil hat so the aliens couldn't read his thoughts?

No! He was perfectly healthy. But . . . maybe he hadn't always been. A break with reality or a sudden mental illness would explain the year and a half of missing days and why the others were so weird around him. But if he had been sick, how did he get over it? Mental illness wasn't like a cold. You didn't just get better by eating chicken soup and drinking OJ.

He knew if he wanted answers, he had to get them on his own, so when the NERDS went home for the day, he padded down the empty hallways to the command center. Though he had never been on a mission in this particular Playground, it wasn't much different from the one at the elementary school. The mission desk had a computer built into it that was activated by hand gestures. He waved his fingers over the circuitry. A moment later a television monitor lowered from the ceiling.

"PLEASE ENTER THE PASSWORD," a computer voice directed as the same words flashed across the screen.

Heathcliff grimaced and said a silent prayer that his nerdy friends had not changed the nerdy password.

"Doctor Who."

"DOCTOR WHO IS INCORRECT ACCESS DENIED PLEASE ENTER THE PASSWORD."

Heathcliff growled. They *had* changed the password! How would he figure out the new one? It was always some reference from science fiction or comic books, but the number of possibilities was staggering. It could be any one of the nine different captains of the *Starship Enterprise*. It could be the name of Luke Skywalker's aunt. It could be the name of the current Green Lantern. Actually, Heathcliff wasn't sure who the current Green Lantern was. He was going to have to catch up on his comics.

Aaargh! He would have to guess. He knew he would only

get three chances before the system locked him out—two, now that he'd blown it with "Doctor Who."

"ENTER THE PASSWORD," the computer commanded again.

Heathcliff closed his eyes tight. Who was the last person to sit at this computer? Matilda! He saw her working on it that morning. Could the password be one of her interests? What was it she liked? . . . Punching people in the face . . . No! Wrestling!

"Rey Mysterio," he said.

"REY MYSTERIO IS INCORRECT ACCESS DENIED PLEASE ENTER THE PASSWORD."

Heathcliff slammed his head on the desk. "What is it? What is the *stupid password*?"

"STUPID PASSWORD IS INCORRECT ACCESS DENIED YOU ARE LOCKED OUT OF THE MAINFRAME FOR THE NEXT TWENTY FOUR HOURS."

The monitor rose toward the ceiling, but Heathcliff refused to let it go. He leaped onto his chair and clung to the screen like a baby chimpanzee nuzzling its mother. He couldn't hold on forever, though, and he fell, cracking his head on the floor tiles. Two hours later, he awoke covered in his own drool and sporting a welt on his head as big as a clementine.

Irritated and sore, he drifted amongst the tables of the

Playground's Science Hub, marveling at its inventions. Occasionally he found himself making subtle corrections to one of the scientists' formulas or an engineering plan—it was one way of helping a team that didn't want his help.

He poked through project after project until he came across a desk covered in junk. Whoever worked here was clearly in over his or her head. Half-finished gizmos littered the workspace, and beneath it miles of tangled cable were tied in hopeless knots. In a cardboard box next to the trash can he found a small, silver orb broken in two like a cracked egg. Wires and gears spilled out of its insides. Abandoned projects could be found all over the Playground, but this one was not just a pile of junk. Heathcliff remembered this device very clearly.

"Benjamin," he said. "How did you get in this box?"

Heathcliff gingerly turned over the robot and marveled at the circuitry inside. Benjamin was beyond extraordinary—a mechanical device with a distinct, almost human, personality. Whoever had created it was much smarter than Heathcliff. In fact, Benjamin was the first piece of technology Heathcliff could remember that truly baffled him. He had once asked about its origins and was told it was top secret. Benjamin was a mystery, just like Heathcliff.

But unlike guessing the passcode, Benjamin wasn't an impossible mystery. It would take time, but Heathcliff was sure he could get the little robot flying again. If the circuit board wasn't too damaged, Benjamin might be able to tell him about the missing months of his life! He shoved Benjamin under his shirt and walked briskly through the science stations, smiling for what felt like the first time in months.

8

38°52' N, 77°6' W

General Savage's face was waiting on the monitor when the principal returned to his office. He braced himself for his boss's rage, but the general wasn't mad. In fact, he looked uncomfortable.

"He wants to talk to the kids."

The principal cocked a curious eyebrow. "Who is *he*?"

"*The* 'he.' The commander in chief."

The principal frowned. "I can't let that happen," he said. "You know that."

The general's thick unibrow swallowed his eyes. "Director, you can't refuse the president of the United States."

"Sir, this organization was created to exist outside the petty politics of whoever is running this country, and for very good reasons. These agents are children. If they are at the command of the president, or the vice president, or Congress, or whomever, it is clear what will happen. They will be yanked out of this school and sent to war zones to fight. Their technology will be stripped and given to soldiers. They will be studied and experimented upon. It will also be disastrous to our mission, which is saving the world—the *entire* world. It's why the team's security clearance is higher than that of the president."

"This is about his daughter," Savage said.

"I am more than happy to talk to him. I can answer any questions he might have. There's no reason for him to meet one of the agents."

"This is not a negotiation. This is an order," Savage barked.

Suddenly, the principal had to resist the incredible desire to grin. He was in a fight—a war of words, but a fight nonetheless—and fighting was what he did best, next to making cherries jubilee. It was the first time since he had become director of the agency that he felt like himself.

"No, sir."

"I can replace you," the general growled.

"And, sir, I can have you arrested."

The general reared back in his chair. "You can *what?*"

"You have violated the law by divulging sensitive materials to individuals who lack the proper clearance."

"I did nothing of the sort!"

"What did you tell the president?"

The general stammered, then growled to cover it up. "I—I told him we had a team of kid spies who were sent to protect his daughter. He doesn't know about the upgrades."

"You have betrayed these children, General."

Savage stared back at him. His face was like a bonfire burning the principal's eyes, but the principal had been in many fires. He would survive this one, too.

"Sir, with all due respect, I encourage you to keep your mouth shut," the principal said.

Savage scowled and the screen went black.

9

When Miss Information was feeling particularly good about one of her evil plans, she baked, so that night she whipped up three apple pies, a pineapple upside-down cake, and a batch of her signature blueberry muffins. The next morning she placed them on a tray and took them to Tessa Lipton, whom she found curled up on the bed, flipping through channels on her TV. Hundreds of tear-soaked tissues littered the room.

"He's not sending the military," she sobbed. "He didn't even call the IRS."

Miss Information sat down on the bed. "Muffin?"

The girl eyed the snacks suspiciously and shook her head.

Miss Information shrugged and set the tray on a nearby table. "Tessa, with the election coming up, your father has to

show the world he's strong. So he's working behind the scenes to recover you without letting the press find out. If he gets you back, he'll tell you not to say anything about it, and you and your family will have to act like it never happened. Right?"

Tessa frowned but nodded.

"No wonder you're a bully."

Tessa's face crinkled with indignation. "I am not a bully."

"Yes, you are, Tessa. You're a certifiable, one hundred percent jerk. You don't have any friends who aren't bullies, and most people are terrified of you. That's the definition of a bully. But it's not your fault. You're like that because you're hurting. Most bullies abuse other people to call attention to their own pain. Sometimes a bully feels insecure about herself, sometimes her victims intimidate her, and sometimes, as in your case, she just wants some love. You intentionally cause problems in the hope that your dad will become more involved in your life. Am I right?"

Tessa sat up and rubbed her swollen eyes. "Yes."

Miss Information smiled beneath her mask. "So you've gotten meaner and meaner to your classmates and teachers but it hasn't worked. I can help you get the attention you want."

"How?"

"Oh, I know a lot about getting attention," Miss Information bragged. "We can make your father regret his choices, and turn him into the daddy you've always wanted. In exchange, you can help me with some of my plans."

"How can I help you?"

"Tessa, being a bully is a skill that requires years of practice to develop. Few bullies ever get past pushing kids on the playground. But *you* . . . you've taken it to a whole new level. Not only are you mean and nasty but you've also found ways to terrorize everyone you've ever met. That, my friend, is a talent I can use."

"What do I have to do?"

Miss Information felt like a fisherman reeling in a trout. All she had to do now was get her catch into the boat.

"You and I will cause a little trouble that will, in turn, cause a little trouble for your dad. Why, it might even cause him to lose the election."

"Lose the election? I can't do that!"

"But, honey, if he loses the election, he'll be out of politics. You'll have him all to yourself."

Tessa sat thinking for a long time.

Miss Information wasn't sure her little fish was still on the line. "I have a team of kids who, like you, need a little attention. All they need is a leader. Someone to boss them around."

A smile crept across Tessa's face.

Miss Information knew she had her now. "And you'll get superpowers."

Tessa frowned. Her eyes went back to looking at the exit.

"Did the Secretary of the Interior put you up to this? He's still angry about the time I called him a tree-hugging hippie."

"You think this is a prank?" Miss Information asked.

Tessa sneered. "I was kidnapped by a lady who wears a skull mask. She wants me to lead a team of kids for her and says she can give me superpowers. You can see why I might think you're crazy."

"I AM NOT CRAZY," Miss Information bellowed. She did not like that word. She was perfectly sane. Tessa had better watch her words. There was always the tiger cage! But then she saw the fear in the girl's eyes, and she took a deep breath to calm herself. "I'm very sorry. Listen, if you want proof that what I'm saying is true, then I'm happy to show you."

She clapped her hands, and a small round hole opened in the wall. Benjy zipped through it and into the room.

"Benjy, I would like Ms. Lipton to meet our team," Miss Information said. "Are they ready?"

"Yes. The upgrade chair you designed this morning has been constructed and is operational. The four operatives you chose have all been through the process successfully."

Miss Information clapped like a happy child. "Have the fire alarm sounded in the school above us. I need their gymnasium."

Benjy chirped and spun. "The alarm has been triggered."

Miss Information pushed a button and the ceiling slid open

to reveal a long dark tunnel. With a loud rumbling noise, the floor beneath them rose like a massive elevator. It went higher and higher, until the room came to an abrupt stop. The four walls fell over as if they were the walls on a house of cards. They had arrived in the middle of an empty basketball court. A basketball rolled across the floor.

"Bring them out, sweetie," Miss Information said to the floating orb.

It spun around and clicked. A door on the far side of the gym opened, and a boy with toadlike features and limp, greasy, shoulder-length hair walked into the gym. His face, clothes, fingernails, and neck were filthy, and he smelled like mildewed towels.

"This is Rash Maver," the orb said. "While some people are wanted criminals, Rash is 'unwanted' in nearly fourteen states due to his lazy approach to personal hygiene. He's been banned in nearly fifty middle schools and more than a few petting zoos. His upgrade allows him to direct a cloud of his own stink to do his bidding. We call him Funk."

"'Upgrade'?" Tessa asked Miss Information.

"It's what gives him his powers—tiny robots, darling." Miss Information pushed a button on the console and leaned into the microphone. "Mr. Maver, can you demonstrate your abilities?"

A rancid green cloud seeped out of the boy's clothes. It

swirled around like a poltergeist, giving off a pungent odor like the smell of rotten eggs slipped into crusty gym socks soaked in spoiled mayonnaise and brown sugar. Funk gestured with his hands and the gas formed different shapes: a cannon firing at a nearby wall, a snarling dog, and an enormous fist. With a flick of his wrist, the mist lifted Funk off the ground and flew him around the gym's rafters.

"That's totally disgusting," Tessa said, gagging.

"Isn't he fun? Wait until you meet the next one," Miss Information said.

Another door swung open and a second boy stepped through. This one had a head of bright white hair and was as skinny as a cornstalk. His finger was buried up his nostril all the way to the knuckle.

"This is Manson Cane," the orb said. "As you can see, he's fond of a peculiar pastime. There are no known photographs of him without his finger in his nose."

Benjy beamed a holographic image in front of them. It was a photo of Manson as a baby. His tiny newborn finger was stuffed in his little baby nose.

"Charming," Tessa grumbled.

"We call him Snot Rocket," Miss Information.

Snot Rocket leaped into action, pressing one finger against his left nostril and blasting enormous globs of mucus out the other. The repulsive rockets crashed into a wall and exploded on contact, demolishing the wall. Mucus missiles from the other nostril allowed him to create elaborate structures made of snot. With a couple of blasts, he created a flight of stairs to race up. A third honk shot a phlegmy tendril across the room, where it stuck like glue. He slid down the booger rope like it was a zip line.

"I'm going to barf!" Tessa cried.

"Clench that belly tight, Ms. Lipton. The next two members are just as obnoxious but not nearly as gross."

A third door opened and a large girl wearing a princess dress and a sparkly tiara appeared. Her pie-shaped face had a sour expression and was bright red.

"This young lady is Tammy Tots. She has a bad reputation and an even louder voice. She's been tossed out of every library and movie theater on the East Coast. I like to call her Loudmouth," Miss Information said as she handed Tessa a pair of earplugs. "You'll need these."

When Tessa's ears were protected, Miss Information pressed the button on her microphone.

"All right, Tammy. You're up."

Loudmouth opened her jaws as wide as possible, and screamed. What she was saying was incoherent but rageful—something about wanting a kitten for Christmas and about a boy named Larry who laughed at her hands. A fierce wind poured from her mouth, ripping up the hardwood floor, tearing down the backboard, and collapsing the bleachers. Miss Information couldn't have been more proud.

"And finally, I present the muscle of our group—Thor Hardwick."

The fourth door in the arena didn't get a chance to open. It was blown apart. As the shattered pieces flew in every direction, a boy as big as a professional wrestler—over six feet tall with a neck like a tree trunk—emerged. His arms and feet were three times the size of a normal person's and twice as long. His knuckles dragged on the floor and sent up a shower of sparks as he walked. He had what looked like a flattop haircut until Tessa realized the top of his head was actually flat. You could land a helicopter on it.

"That can't be a child!" Tessa said. "Does he have a beard?"

"Thor comes from a long line of lumberjacks and pro wrestlers . . . and that's just the women in his family. He's brutally strong and psychotically violent, to boot. I was going to give him a code name, but when your parents name you Thor, you really can't do better than that."

Thor punched a wall and it came down in a mighty explosion. He smiled and took a bow as if he'd just done a magic trick. Then he grabbed the rolling basketball and popped it with one squeeze.

Beneath her mask, Miss Information was beaming proudly. She had a great team, and Tessa would make it complete. Plus,

Tessa was exactly what she needed to lure her enemies into the open. And when they came, she would crush them like bugs.

"Tessa, I can give you powers like I gave them."

Tessa cringed. "Just like *them*?"

"Slightly less gross. I hope," Miss Information said. "I know you have your doubts, but no one has given these kids a chance in this world. They need someone like you—someone with your unique ability to motivate. They need a leader."

"I don't want my dad to get hurt. I just don't want him to be president anymore."

"Understood."

"OK, I'm in," Tessa said.

"Fantastic! Welcome to the Brotherhood of Unstoppable Liars, Lowlifes, and Intimidating Enemies of Society!"

"That's what you want to call us?" Tessa muttered. "Shouldn't it be something scary and intimidating?"

"How about if we just call you the BULLIES?"

"The BULLIES," Tessa said, savoring the name like a spoonful of ice cream. "I like it."

"Muffin?" Miss Information asked, offering another treat from her tray.

This time Tessa picked a muffin and took a bite.

END TRANSMISSION.

TOP SECRET DOSSIER
CODE NAME: BREEZY
REAL NAME: NIGEL PUNJAB
YEARS ACTIVE: 2005-09
CURRENT OCCUPATION:
OWNER OF NIGEL'S
HOUSE OF NICETIES

HISTORY: NIGEL'S FAMILY OWNED A VERY POPULAR INDIAN RESTAURANT SPECIALIZING IN SPICY DISHES OF LENTILS, POTATOES, AND CAULIFLOWER. SO NIGEL HAD INTENSE AND OFTEN FRIGHTENING GASTRIC ISSUES. IN FACT, THE BOY WAS SO GASSY, HE BARELY NEEDED ANY NANOBYTES TO ENHANCE AN ALREADY POWERFUL POOT. HE WAS AN INVALUABLE MEMBER OF THE TEAM, SINGLE-HANDEDLY STOPPING THE INFAMOUS FLOWER POWER CRIMINAL RING. NIGEL RETIRED SHORTLY AFTER HIS FAMILY CLOSED THE RESTAURANT AND OPENED A HALLMARK CARD STORE.

UPGRADE: BREEZY'S UPGRADES
TURNED HIS ALREADY FORMIDABLE
FARTS INTO HOUSE-LEVELING BLASTS
OF WIND AND STINK. MANY OF HIS
FARTS WERE CAPABLE OF REACHING
AN F2 LEVEL ON THE NATIONAL
WEATHER SERVICE'S TORNADO RATING.

LEVEL 4
ACCESS GRANTED

BEGIN TRANSMISSION:

10

38°52' N, 77°6' W

Ruby woke the next morning with
her parents and baby brother hovering over her bed. They
looked sweaty and nervous. Even Truman the dog looked
anxious. He buried his furry head under her blanket.

"They're here," her mother whispered. She looked terrified.

Ruby could hear someone pounding on the front door.

"Who?"

"Our family," she said. Her father pressed a finger to his
lips. "Be quiet. They'll hear you and come after us."

"They're early! I haven't finished the bathroom schedule or
color-coded the snacks!" Ruby whispered.

"They took us by surprise." Her father was actually
whimpering. His panicked eyes darted from the door to her
windows.

Ruby heard someone knocking on the back door.

"Just stay quiet, and maybe they'll go away and come back later," he said.

Without warning, a mob appeared outside Ruby's window and gaped at her family. They smiled and laughed and tapped on the glass.

"Surprise!" they cried.

Ruby's mother cringed and opened the window.

"You're early," she said.

"We couldn't stand to wait another second," said Grandma Rose.

"Oh, Ruby, you're so grown up!" said Aunt Suzi.

"Hey, Rubester! What grade are you in now?" Uncle Kevin shouted.

"Sarah, you look like you've put on some weight."

"I hope whatever we're eating tonight is kosher."

"Can we come inside? I gotta use the can."

"I have to get out of these shoes."

"I call the bathroom for the next half hour."

"Sarah, I noticed a Christmas tree in the window but not a menorah."

Aunt Laura poked her head through the window. "Francis, you *are* celebrating Christmas, right? It's not just the candles and the little wooden tops this year?"

"Laura, they're called dreidels," Ruby's father said. "And yes, we celebrate Christmas. We also celebrate Hanukkah."

"Of course you celebrate Hanukkah!" Grandpa Saul chimed in. "Who needs a holiday that is only one day long? Hanukkah lasts eight days! It's simple math. More presents, right?"

"Yes, every kid in the world dreams of a handful of stale chocolate coins," Aunt Suzi said.

"All right, let's not start the Battle of the Best Holiday. You've only been here five minutes," Sarah said.

"Technically, we're not here until you let us inside," said Cousin Finn.

Ruby's family shared a brief but conspiratorial look that said, *We could just close the window and go back to bed*, but then Sarah flinched.

"Of course. Come around to the front door and we'll let you in," she said.

"Traitor," Ruby grumbled.

"At least you get to go to school," Sarah said. "Your father and I took the day off to get everything ready. Now we're stuck."

"We all need to work together. Mom, call the deli on Hamilton and get some bagels and lox over here for breakfast. When you're done, start pouring coffee and juice. Dad, I need you on pancake duty."

"OK. Where's the batter?"

"The cabinet over the stove, second shelf, next to the flour. Blueberries are in the crisper, bottom shelf of the refrigerator. Syrup is in the condiment caddy on the door. If you get lost, there are charts posted everywhere, or you can check the family guide I made that's attached to a chain swinging from a kitchen table leg. I'm on toilet paper duty. If Grandpa Saul called dibs on the bathroom, we need to be prepared. Truman and Noah, you've got the toughest job of all—you have to be cute. Turn on the adorable, and maybe everyone will forget how much they can't stand one another. Any questions?"

Little Noah burped. *"Gooby-moo-moo."*

Ruby clapped her hands. "Good. Team Peet—let's do this!"

Ruby's family sprang into action.

Soon the members of her extended family were filing into the house like clowns stepping out of a tiny car. When hats, coats, gloves, and galoshes were taken, hugs, kisses, and pats on the back delivered, and updates on everyone's bad knees, agita, and high blood pressure were announced, the family eased into a slightly tense camaraderie fueled by food. Ruby had learned the hard way that these two, loud, obnoxious clans were a lot easier to manage when they had snacks in their mouths.

According to her parents, the tense relationship between Sarah's and Francis's families had started right away. For Sarah and Francis, it was love at first sight; but for their families, it was a nightmare of biblical proportions. Francis was a Boston-born Protestant raised by a huge family of big, strapping folk who loved to eat, shout about the Red Sox, and argue with one another in a way most people might find threatening but that they referred to as "chatting." Sarah's family was Jewish and from Long Island, New York. Their loudness rivaled that of the Peet family, plus they were die-hard Yankees fans and claimed to be freezing no matter what temperature the thermostat was set at. Sarah and Francis tried to accommodate everyone with a Christmas tree and a menorah, but each year someone would say something that offended someone else and all the holiday cheer would turn into a holiday fight.

"Why was Ruby still in bed when we showed up? The sun has been out for fifteen minutes," Grandpa Tom grumbled. "When I was a kid, it was my job to wake up the roosters so they would crow. She's wasting the day."

"Ruby has a lot of things on her plate at school," her father explained. "She needs all the rest she can get."

"Too many extracurricular activities aren't good. Let a kid be a kid, I always say," said Uncle Kevin.

Cousin Leaf chuckled. "I know what she's doing up so late. She's writing love letters to boys."

"Don't tease her, Leaf," Aunt Denise said, taking the baby from Sarah. "Look at this beautiful boy."

Yes, do your job, Noah. Take the attention off me, please, thought Ruby.

There was a knock at the door and she heard Uncle Eddie shout that he'd get it. A moment later he returned. "There's a man here to see Ruby."

"Me? Who is it?"

"He says he's your principal," Uncle Eddie replied. "Are you in trouble, kid?"

"Ruby?" her father asked suspiciously.

"Um, no, he's just very dedicated," Ruby lied as she snatched her coat. "It's probably about the winter dance. He wants me to be on the decorating committee."

Moments later, she was outside on the front step, talking to the principal. A curious relative's face peered out of every window of her home.

"Looks like you've got a full house today, huh?" the principal said, staring at the prying eyes.

"Jewish mother, Protestant father—all of Israel and England is here," Ruby explained.

"It's hard to believe they get along," the principal said.

"Really hard to believe because they don't. So . . . what's going on?" Ruby asked, cutting to the chase. "Is there news on Tessa?"

"No, not a peep."

"Then why not use the com-link?"

"Because I didn't want anyone else to hear what I'm going to tell you. We have a huge problem," the principal said. "I think we're about to be exposed."

"Exposed? By whom?"

"Savage," he said. "I got a call on the secure line. He told the president about the team. Not about the upgrades—not yet—but the big guy knows we exist."

The news felt like a blow to her belly. "What are we going to do?"

"I don't know. That's why we're going to talk to Alexander Brand."

"Are you going to ask him to come back?"

"No," the principal said. "He won't. But I think he'll be able to tell me what to do."

Ruby felt a little guilty leaving her folks alone with the mob they called family, but not *that* guilty. She grabbed her things, pulled a hat over her head, and climbed into the principal's Jeep. Soon, they were driving southwest along a scenic highway lined with snowy fir trees. After an hour, they turned onto an old country road that ran next to a crystal lake and then past tiny little cottages with ribbons of smoke escaping from their chimneys. The farther they drove, the more breathtaking the scenery. Ruby felt like they had entered a beautiful painting.

Then came more turns that forced them to make a few stops and reroutes. Ruby and the principal were ready to give up when they suddenly stumbled upon a mailbox hidden behind a thorny bush. The principal stopped the Jeep, got out, and shoved the branches aside. The mailbox had a name painted in red: A. BRAND.

They drove up the overgrown driveway path made from years of tire tracks and coasted beneath a canopy of leafless trees until a tiny log cabin appeared on the shore of the lake. As soon as the principal cut the Jeep's engine, he and Ruby's eardrums were assaulted by what sounded like the painful death throes of a very large animal.

"What *is* that?" Ruby asked.

The principal shrugged. "Could be anything. A moose . . . a bear. We should be careful. The most dangerous animal is the one that's dying."

The two spies crept around the corner of the house and immediately spotted the source of the noise. At the end of a long dock sat a lone figure who appeared to be strangling a cat. Ruby took off her glasses and wiped the smudges off the lenses, then slipped them back on to get a better look. She could see the man was not hurting an animal but rather playing an oboe—badly. When he blew on the woodwind's reed, it emitted a sound like a duck exploding inside a kazoo.

His screeches terrified the lake birds, who flew away, panicked.

"Um . . . ," Ruby said, at a loss for words to describe what she was seeing.

"A broken heart can do strange things to a man," the principal explained. "Brand took Lisa's betrayal particularly hard. He had some loss when he was a kid—his brother was killed in the air force, and he'd built a lot of walls around himself. I suspect the librarian was chipping away at them before she went nuts."

"I don't think Ms. Holiday was the only one to go nuts," Ruby said as another note soured the air.

They walked across the lawn, past the house, and onto the dock, where they stood waiting for Brand's atrocious concert to end. When the last jagged note was played, the former hero set his instrument down on his lap as if its weight was more than he could bear.

"How did you find me?" he said without turning to face them.

"We're spies," Ruby said. "But I suspect we could have just asked who was out here torturing a goose."

Brand growled and turned in his chair. "The oboe is the dignified gentleman of the woodwind instruments!"

His face was thin and covered in a long, ratty beard filled with flecks of food and dead leaves, and his once perfectly coiffed hair was long and greasy. He wore a filthy shirt spattered with stains, and he smelled like an old catcher's mitt left out in the rain.

"I'm trying to teach myself to play," Brand said. "It's not something you pick up overnight."

"How long have you been trying to teach yourself?" the principal asked.

"On and off? Ten years."

Brand picked up his instrument and blasted another ragged note into the air. Somewhere, a bear roared angrily.

"We need to talk to you," Ruby said.

"No."

"No?"

"To whatever you want to ask," he said.

"Shouldn't you let us ask the question first?" the principal said.

"No."

Ruby scratched her belly. She was allergic to stubbornness.

"Alex, we are barely surviving," the principal said. "Savage is about to tell the president our secrets, the kids haven't been in a classroom in months, and your ex-girlfriend is kicking our behinds. Every day, five twelve-year-old kids have to stop another end-of-the-world scenario. They've been depending on luck more than they should, and yesterday the luck ran out. Lisa kidnapped the president's daughter."

"She'll bring Tessa back once she realizes what a brat she is. Serves her right."

"What do I do about Savage?" the principal asked.

"Prepare for the worst."

"He'd listen to you."

"I said no."

Ruby stepped forward. "So you'll let old bullet-head tell the government about us? You know what that means, right?"

"If they come, run," Brand said. "Destroy the Playground. The self-destruct password is 'Maxwell Smart.'"

"You're also turning your back on Ms. Holiday!"

Brand turned to face Ruby. His eyes were full of anguish.

"Ms. Holiday is sick," Ruby said, her voice shaking. "She must still be infected with the villain virus, and you walked away from her. She needs your help!"

Brand shook his head. "Ms. Holiday is not suffering from any virus. She was spying on us."

"That's not true!"

"Yes, it is, Ruby," Brand said. "When she went rogue, I wanted to believe that she was sick or being manipulated. But we searched her house. We found fifteen different passports, seven different birth certificates, and detailed notes on the Playground, you kids, and me. The Lisa Holiday we know is really Viktoriya Deprankova of Novosibirsk, Siberia. She's the

daughter of exiled political activists. When she was fifteen, she robbed her parents, stole a car, and drove it cross-country with a professional thug named Lars Corsica. They got married, but when they were arrested for the stolen car, Lars told the Russian police his bride was responsible for a dozen crimes *he* had actually committed. Viktoriya was sentenced to fifteen years in prison. After the verdict, she was approached by a member of the Russian secret service, who offered her a way out of jail—she could become a spy."

"You're saying she was a double agent?" Ruby said.

"They trained her to be one of us. She learned English, went to college, was even a cheerleader, and then a librarian—as American as apple pie."

"But I thought we were getting along with the Russians," Ruby said.

"We are, but old habits die hard," the principal said. "I'm sure we have deep-cover spies in their country, too."

"Regardless, she wasn't real and neither was our relationship," Brand said. "Everything was a lie and I was too stupid to see it. That's why I can't help you. I can't trust my instincts anymore."

"Did you know this?" Ruby asked the principal.

The principal nodded.

"OK, so she's a bad guy," Ruby said. "That's another good reason to help us. You can't just run off to some cabin and grow a hipster beard and go *whah! whah! whah!* on your stupid oboe!"

"I'm not going to be lectured by someone whose biggest problem is whether her mom is going to get her to soccer practice on time."

Brand turned back to the lake. Ruby couldn't believe it, but the bravest man she had ever known had thrown in the towel.

Frustrated, she marched back to the Jeep.

"Well, that's that," the principal said when he got into the driver's seat. He started the engine and drove back down the overgrown driveway.

On the drive back, Ruby gazed out at the countryside and rubbed her swollen feet. She was allergic to disappointment.

11

Tessa followed Miss Information through the halls of her huge underground lair until they reached a thick steel door labeled UPGRADE ROOM. She watched her new boss place her hands on a green glass screen next to the door. The glass flashed, and a moment later the door slid open.

The room was completely empty except for a silver podium.

"What's this thing?" Tessa asked.

"This is where the magic happens, and that's the magic wand," Miss Information said.

She pressed a blue button on the podium. Red laser lights danced across the walls and swarmed over Tessa's body like bees on a flower.

"What's going on?" she asked.

Miss Information grinned. "You're being scanned for your biggest strength."

"STRENGTH DETECTED SUBJECT IS TWO-FACED," a voice said.

"Hey!" Tessa cried. "Is this some kind of joke?"

The robotic voice ignored her. **"SUBJECT TAKES GREAT PLEASURE IN DECEPTION SUBJECT IS A BACKSTABBER SUBJECT IS A CHAMELEON SUBJECT NEEDS MORE THAN ONE FACE SUBJECT NEEDS MANY FACES PREPARE FOR UPGRADE."**

"Here we go," Miss Information said. "I'm going to step out and monitor from the hall."

"Wait! I—"

But the woman was already through the door.

An observation panel opened in the wall, and Tessa could see her new boss in her bizarre mask waving to her like Tessa was about to ride her first roller coaster.

"INITIATE UPGRADE?"

The question repeated itself over and over, but Tessa could not answer.

"If you want to do this, you need to say the word *begin*," Ms. Holiday instructed. Her voice came through a speaker mounted on the wall.

"What if I don't want to?"

"There's nothing to worry about, Tessa!" Miss Information said. "This is going to help you get your daddy back."

"INITIATE UPGRADE?"

The woman could be a nutcase. Or this could be an elaborate revenge from the director of the CIA; he was still mad about that wedgie she gave him. But . . . what if this was real? What if this woman was really offering Tessa her greatest wish? She might look like a fool later, but it was worth the risk.

"Yes, begin!" Tessa cried.

Tubes attached to dozens of fearsome tools dropped from the ceiling and wrapped themselves around her body. She was yanked off the floor and held aloft like a fly caught in a spiderweb.

"Um, is this normal?" Tessa asked.

Miss Information gave her a thumbs-up through the window.

Several large hypodermic needles sprung from the ends of the tubes, which moved dangerously close to Tessa's neck. "I've changed my mind. I don't want to do this!" she said.

"Ruby, please, calm down. This will be over soon, and afterwards we'll go out for frozen yogurt. Do you like frozen yogurt? What a silly question. Everyone loves frozen yogurt!"

"My name is Tessa," she shouted.

"Of course it is," Miss Information said. She seemed dazed. "What did I just call you?"

"Ruby," Tessa said.

The woman clamped her hands on her head and buckled over as if hit with the worst headache anyone had ever experienced. Tessa watched her fall to her knees and cry out.

One of the needles went into the side of Tessa's temple, and she felt like her head was on fire. As the room turned black, she heard her new boss say, "This part might hurt a little. Just keep thinking about that yogurt, sweetheart."

Tessa didn't know how long she'd been asleep—a day? Maybe two? All she knew was that when she woke up, she felt different. Her skin felt tingly and alive. It was as if every pore was suddenly aware of its own existence. It felt very good, but it scared her, too. What had that machine done to her?

Miss Information barged into the room. "Wakey, wakey! Let's give these superpowers a test-drive!" she said.

Tessa sat up and narrowed her eyes at the woman. Who was behind that mask? What did this woman really look like? What was she hiding?

Miss Information pulled Tessa to her feet and dragged her to a mirror. "Let's see you do it."

"Do what?"

"The thing! The power! With your face!"

"I don't know what that machine did to me, and I certainly don't know how to do anything," Tessa snapped.

"Geez, do I have to do everything around here?" Miss Information cried. With lightning-fast hands, she reached over and pulled on Tessa's nose.

"Hey!" Tessa cried. "What are you, seven years old? Go play Got Your Nose with someone else!"

Miss Information pointed at the mirror. "Look."

Tessa screamed. Loudly. Her nose was now where her chin used to be!

"Crazy, huh?" Miss Information said. She stood over Tessa's shoulder, marveling at the grotesque change. "I read the data on your nanobytes. Those little robots let you manipulate your face anyway you want. You can actually sculpt your skin to look like other people, too. Try it!"

"Who?"

"Who cares? Just pick someone!"

Tessa closed her eyes and thought about the people in her life. Then her hands went to work, twisting and turning her features as if they were Play-Doh. Her nose, lips, skin—even her eyeballs—were all soft and pliable, and, oddly enough, all the pulling and twisting didn't hurt. When she was done, she took a step back and looked in the mirror. Her math teacher,

Mr. Donaldson, stared back at her. His beady eyes and scowling mouth were perfect matches. She even duplicated his famous curled lip of contempt and the single ever-present nose hair that waved like a flag from his right nostril.

She screamed again.

"That's amazing, Tessa!" Ms. Holiday said. "Try someone else."

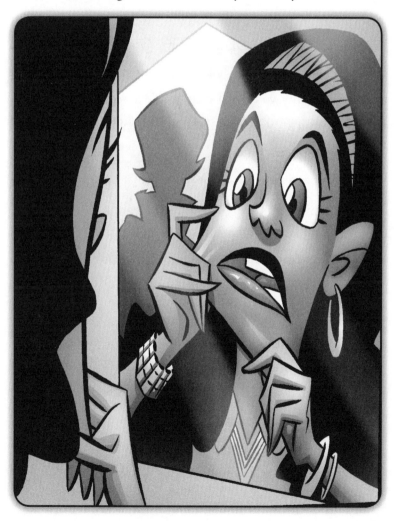

She did as she was told, filled with both dread and curiosity. In quick succession she turned herself into Secret Service Agent Dan Holbrooke, Holly the White House chef, and even George Washington from the portrait that hung in the Oval Office. Her nanobytes were incredible. Not only had they turned her face into clay, they allowed her to adapt her eye color, skin tone, and even hair color.

Miss Information clapped happily. "With a little practice you should be able to do your whole body. You can change your height and weight—why, you might even be able to reproduce smells."

A few quick twists and Tessa had her old face back. "Um, I'm going to pass."

"*What?* Best power ever!" Miss Information cried.

"It's disgusting. I want something else."

"The upgrade machine takes your greatest strength and makes it stronger. This is perfect for you! Don't tell me you wanted to fly or something dumb like that?"

"Flying wouldn't be so bad."

"Yeah, freezing to death while bugs fly into your mouth," the woman said. "That's horrible. Any kid with an egg can knock you out of the sky. Tessa, with your face you can be anyone you want to be. Think of the trouble you can cause! You could rob a bank by pretending to be the branch manager. You could steal a jet by changing your face to look like the pilot!"

"How is this going to get my dad's attention?"

"Imagine what you could do if you were the president of the United States."

Tessa looked in the mirror and twisted her features until she looked just like her father. A million naughty ideas floated into her head. She could stop him from being reelected, and then she'd have him all to herself.

"I see you're getting it," Miss Information said, giggling. She clamped a bracelet onto Tessa's wrist and snapped it closed. "While you were out I had the science team build this hologram machine. It will project any set of clothes you can imagine onto your body and totally help sell your transformations. Now, you said you wanted to get your dad's attention, right? Let's get started."

"Now?"

"There's no time like the present," Miss Information said as she led Tessa out of her room and through a maze of hallways. They emerged into a space as big as a private plane hangar, but there were no planes parked inside, just a rusty yellow school bus. Standing in front of it was her team—the BULLIES. She looked them up and down and couldn't help frowning. These kids were the biggest bunch of misfits she'd ever seen.

"Ta-da!" Miss Information said. "I call it 'The School Bus.'"

"It *is* a school bus," Tessa said.

"Not exactly," Miss Information replied. She clicked a button on her key chain and the wheels folded upward replaced by rockets. Soon, the ancient bucket of rust was hovering five feet off the ground.

Tessa shrugged. "It's got potential."

"There's more! BULLIES, hop on board," Miss Information said.

The children boarded the bus one by one. A strange man sat behind the steering wheel. He was a mountain of muscles with crazy white hair, a wide chin, a dead eye, and a silver hook for a hand. He was also wearing white orthopedic shoes and a smock with bright blue flowers on it.

"Kids, this is the lunch lady."

"Lunch lady? He's a bus driver wearing a muumuu," Loudmouth shouted.

"He's not a lady, either," Funk said.

"Actually, my name is the Antagonist, but—"

"YOU'RE THE LUNCH LADY!" Miss Information roared. "DON'T MAKE ME REGRET BREAKING YOU OUT OF FEDERAL PRISON, PAL. I CAN PUT YOU BACK THERE IN A FLASH. YOU GOT IT?"

The man with the hook lowered his head and nodded. "I got it," he said quietly.

Tessa watched the woman's outburst with concern. This was

the second unpredictable rant she'd witnessed. Miss Information was obviously mentally ill—people didn't wear masks with skulls on them because they were healthy—but just how crazy was she? A moment later she found out. Her new boss sat in a center seat next to a scarecrow wearing a black tuxedo. She cuddled up to it as if it were her boyfriend.

"This is so awkward," Miss Information said in a conspiratorial tone.

"What?" Tessa said, trying to pretend everything was fine.

"The lunch lady and I used to be engaged. That's before I met Alex here," she said, caressing the straw man's hay-filled face.

"Where to?" the lunch lady shouted.

"We're going to Tessa's house—1600 Pennsylvania Avenue. You might have heard of it. It's called the White House."

Tessa swallowed hard. Her greatest wishes were about to come true, and she owed it all to a lunatic in a mask smooching a scarecrow. She suddenly felt very nauseous.

12

When Ruby and the principal got back to school, they were rushed on board the School Bus. The platform the superjet was resting upon was already rising through the gym floor before either of them was given a clue as to the nature of the emergency.

"Does anyone want to tell me where we're going?" the principal said as the rocket shot through the open ceiling. "So I know where to steer this thing?"

"Put in coordinates for Lake Mead, Nevada," Matilda said. "We're going to the Hoover Dam. And it wouldn't hurt to floor it."

"What's happening at the Hoover Dam?" Ruby asked.

"Robot destruction!" Flinch bellowed while beating on his chest.

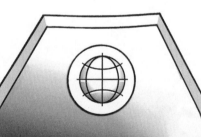

"I suppose we can blame them on Miss Information?" Ruby asked.

"Take a look for yourself. Our surveillance team caught this fifteen minutes ago," Duncan said. He typed something on the mission deck keyboard, and in the monitors Ruby saw men unloading heavy wooden crates from a truck parked on a dusty road near a lake. When they opened one of the crates, something from a science fiction movie hopped out. It was about the size of a sheepdog but strutted around on two chicken-like hind legs. Its head was oval and black with a white skull pattern. It shrieked, flew twenty feet into the air on metallic wings, then fell back to the ground with a thud.

"Chickenbots," Duncan said. "There's ten of them, and they're marching toward the dam."

"Three minutes, kids," the principal shouted from the cockpit.

"You better suit up," Duncan said to Ruby. He handed her a duffle bag full of black clothing.

Matilda opened the rocket's hatch and the wind blasted into the cabin.

Ruby peered out into the great blue oblivion as she pulled the flight suit over her school clothes.

"Um, aren't we forgetting something very important . . . like parachutes?"

"If you pull the cord on your waist, you'll release something better—wings!" Duncan shouted over the noise.

"Wings?" Ruby cried.

Duncan sighed. "Folks, we're all given instruction manuals for this stuff. Am I the only one who reads them?"

Jackson nodded. "Yes, you are."

"This is the ALZ-14 Aerial Assault Flight Suit. You pull the cord and two wings will extend from your shoulders, turning you into a human bird."

"One minute!" the principal cried from the cockpit.

"And don't forget the electromagnetic-pulse gloves," Duncan said as he extended his hand to point out his special glove. It was black and covered in thin, silver wires that connected to a red disk on the palm. Ruby knew what an electromagnetic pulse could do to electronics. One blast and those robots would stop working.

"All right, kids! We're over the target!" the principal shouted.

Flinch slurped down one very long red licorice rope like a little kid might eat a strand of spaghetti. "Fight robots! *Aggghhhooo!*" he cried as he leaped out of the rocket.

Soon Ruby and the others were plummeting toward earth at skin-stretching speeds. Below her, and getting bigger by the second, was the Hoover Dam, one of the most impressive structures ever built by human hands. A long time ago, when

Ruby actually went to classes, she had written a report on it. It was built between 1931 and 1936 during the Great Depression, and it provided electricity for cities hundreds of miles away. It was 660 feet wide, stood more than 726 feet tall, and held back 9.2 trillion gallons of water. It was so massive that some said an asteroid might not even topple it. If Ruby knew how tough the dam was, Miss Information would certainly have to know. She was a librarian, after all. Even if these chickenbots managed to destroy it, the nearest big town was 125 miles away, which meant it wasn't an imminent threat to anyone's safety. So what was Miss Information's plan?

When they were a quarter-mile over the dam, Ruby could squint and see tiny red explosions on the surface of the dam's wall. She guessed the robots were already hard at work on their task. She checked her EMP glove to make sure it was powered and then squeezed her nose.

"All right, Duncan, I'm ready to turn into Big Bird."

Duncan giggled. Gadgets always made him happy. Explaining how they worked was as fun as Disney World. "Do your best to level out of a nosedive. You want to be parallel with the horizon when you launch the wings."

Ruby and the others did as they were told.

"Now, pull the rip cord and the wings will extend. Once they unfold, your fall will slow, and ropes will drop from each wing. Grab them to help you steer. Just remember two things: One, don't get too close to the ground, and two, don't get too close to the dam."

"*Splat!*" Flinch cried.

"Splat," Duncan said.

"All right, here I go." With the wind slamming into her stomach, Ruby pulled the cord and felt the wings unfold. Her fall came to an abrupt stop. She found the ropes Duncan mentioned and snatched them both. At first, the slightest pull sent her flailing, but she quickly learned how to make subtle adjustments. She could fly! With a slight tug to the right she soared along the dam, approached one of the robots, and aimed her glove. It fired with a screech. Unfortunately, she missed, and the skull-faced robot was undamaged.

"Fudge!" she growled, steering back for another pass. This time she pulled closer to get a better shot, but as she approached, her target turned and blasted a stream of fire directly at her. She narrowly avoided getting a barbecued face and had to pat out a small fire on her leg. Worse, she missed her second shot.

"Gluestick, this is a lot harder than you described," she said over the com-link.

"I agree," Flinch said. "I gave up and went old-school."

Ruby scanned the sky for the hyper hero. She found him dive-bombing one of the robots. He walloped it with a power punch and it exploded in a blast of fire and steel. What was left fell into the river below.

"The wings were getting in my way, too," Matilda said, rushing past Ruby, fueled by her rocket-powered inhalers. When she got close to one of the robots, she destroyed it with a fiery blast.

"C'mon, Pufferfish. You're missing all the fun," Braceface said. Two long tentacles made from his orthodontic implants emerged from his mouth, snatched a couple of Miss Information's robots, and smashed them together. They crumbled and joined the others in the river.

"This is too easy," Gluestick said, soaring past Ruby and firing his EMP device at one of the robots. There was no explosion. With all its internal electronics fried, it just fell off the wall and into the water.

"You better hurry while there's one left," Flinch said, kicking another robot so hard that it slammed into the side of the dam and exploded.

Ruby pulled on the wings' ropes to head back toward the metallic fiends. When she was close, she raised her EMP glove and fired. The robot turned its head to blast her, but this time she delivered an exact hit and it froze with a jerk. Then it fell off the dam and tumbled end over end into the water below.

"Only three left, people," Ruby said.

"This was hardly worth the trip," Matilda said, aiming her inhaler at one of the remaining robots. A hot blue flame came out of it and melted a hole in the robot's skull-painted head. It exploded like the others.

Ruby agreed. This *was* too easy. The chickenbots were barely hurting the dam wall at all, and aside from the flamethrowing they weren't putting up much of a fight. Not all of Miss Information's schemes were brilliant, but this one seemed downright dumb.

"Uh-oh," Gluestick said.

"What's 'Uh-oh'?" Ruby asked. "I hate 'Uh-oh.'"

"They're doing something," Flinch said.

Ruby looked at the three remaining robots. Their eyes had turned red, and a loud, pulsing beat came from within their metal chests. It sounded like a countdown.

Suddenly, Ruby's fingers felt swollen and her neck itched like crazy. She was allergic to bombs, and even more allergic to getting caught in an explosion.

"Everyone!" she cried. "Go!" But she was too late. The three remaining chickenbots exploded at the same time. Ruby and the other agents were thrown backward. Her wings were shredded, making it impossible to stay airborne. She crashed into the cold, churning river below. As she sank deep into the water's darkness, struggling to hold her breath, she unfastened what was left of her flight suit and swam with all her might toward the dim light above her. She broke the surface and gasped for air, and saw all of her teammates doing the same.

"Is everyone OK?" Ruby gasped.

"It was some kind of concussion bomb," Gluestick said. "Look, it didn't even hurt the dam."

Ruby turned and eyed the surface where the robots had once clung. All that remained was a charred stain.

"This doesn't make any sense," she said. "What kind of lousy diabolical plan was that?"

Suddenly, all five of the NERDS sneezed. The com-link was open and Heathcliff was waiting.

"Guys, we need you back here pronto," he said. "There's trouble at the White House."

"How much money do you want to put on it being Miss Information?" Jackson asked.

"These stupid robots were just to keep us busy," Ruby said. "She wanted us far away from Washington, D.C., and we fell for it. Heathcliff, tell the principal to pick us up pronto. We're going to kick some serious supervillain butt."

END TRANSMISSION.

TOP SECRET DOSSIER
CODE NAME: MOUSE
REAL NAME: ABRAHAM SHRIVEL
YEARS ACTIVE: 1990-95
CURRENT OCCUPATION:
PROFESSIONAL WRESTLER

HISTORY: ABRAHAM WAS SMALL FOR HIS AGE. BY THE TIME HE WAS TEN, HE WAS STILL ONLY THREE FEET TALL. IN THE FOURTH GRADE, HE SPENT NEARLY FIVE MONTHS BURIED BENEATH HIS CLASSMATES' COATS. BECOMING A MEMBER OF NERDS INCREASED HIS CONFIDENCE TENFOLD, AND HE CAN NOW BE SEEN WRESTLING FOR THE WWE AS "THE STUD."

UPGRADE: ABRAHAM'S UPGRADES CHANGED HIS CELLULAR STRUCTURE SO THAT HE COULD SHRINK TO ANY SIZE-EVEN

MICROSCOPIC. BEING ABLE TO SLIP
UNDER ANY DOOR, INTO ANY SAFE
LOCK, OR THROUGH A KEYHOLE MADE
HIM AN INVALUABLE AGENT.

LEVEL 5
ACCESS GRANTED

BEGIN TRANSMISSION:

13

38°53' N, 77°2' W

"Kids, if you're going to cause a ruckus, start with a grand entrance," Miss Information said as the School Bus slammed through the cast-iron fence that surrounded the White House. The bus tore across the lawn before skidding to a halt by the front door.

"Are you nuts?" Snot Rocket shouted as he peered out the window. "That's the White House! There will be guards everywhere. Oh, look, here they come now."

Miss Information peeked out her window. Snot Rocket was right. Secret Service agents in dark suits were crawling out of every nook and cranny. They were joined by a company of soldiers all carrying large weapons. The bus was surrounded within seconds.

"What were you thinking?" Loudmouth bellowed.

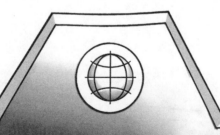

"I was thinking we'd try your powers out," Miss Information said. "And fulfill a promise to Tessa at the same time. This is going to cause her dad all kinds of hassle."

"Couldn't we have started off with a shopping mall or an old folks' home?" Funk asked. "We need practice before we do something crazy like this."

Snot Rocket dug his finger into his nose. "We're all going to jail. They're going to throw us in a dark hole and never let us out."

"No one is going to jail, silly," Miss Information said. "Look at those guards. They're just regular people. Now look at yourselves. You're experienced bullies with unstoppable superpowers. You're machines of chaos! Besides, it's not like you haven't done this before. You guys have been a team for years."

Tessa turned to face her. "This is our *first time*."

Miss Information felt like someone had unleashed a hive of angry hornets inside her head. She thought she might barf and had to hold on to the seat in front of her to make sure she didn't pass out. It's what happened when she got confused, and lately, she was confused a lot. Of course, she knew Tessa was right. This *was* the BULLIES' first mission. But her memories kept getting jumbled with the wild, unsettling dreams she had at night, where she was a librarian who helped a group of kids save the world. She was in love with a man who had amazing hair, and she wore an awful lot of cardigans. But those kids in her dreams were her worst nightmare in the real world. They called themselves NERDS and were responsible for ruining all of her plans. Why was she confusing the two? Was there something wrong with her?

"OK, Tessa 'Code Name to Be Decided' Lipton. What's the plan?" she asked, forcing the fog from her mind.

The girl blinked back at her.

"Tessa, this is *your* show. What do you think we should do to get your daddy's attention?"

She stared blankly at the White House.

"Tessa, a good leader can come up with a winning plan no matter what the situation. We're here and we're surrounded. What should we do?"

"Um . . ."

Miss Information tried to be patient with her. She was probably just suffering from first-time supervillain jitters.

"OK, listen up. As as you can see, we're surrounded," Miss Information continued. "If we try to get off this bus, they will arrest us. Luckily, we have someone with us who can change her appearance to look like someone very important—someone like the president of the United States. Isn't that right, Tessa?" Tessa went to work twisting her face, until she looked like the identical twin of her father. Her holographic projector built a sharp blue suit just like the one her father wore. The rest of the team stared at her in awe.

"See? What did I tell you? Coolest power ever!" Miss Information said, helping Tessa out of her seat and toward the front of the bus, where the Antagonist sat in his kitchen smock. He opened the door with his silver hook and wished them luck.

Immediately, the guards and soldiers lowered their weapons.

"Mr. President," one of the guards said to Tessa. "We had no idea it was you. Where is your security detail, sir?"

"Um . . . we got a flat tire, so they stayed with the car," Tessa said in as deep a voice as she could muster. "And these fine, upstanding children offered me a ride home. Sorry if we've caused any problems."

"Perhaps we should get you inside."

"Good thinking. Kids, who wants a tour?" Tessa asked.

The guard shook his head. "Sir, I'm sure we could schedule something, but the children need to be screened in advance."

"Oh, c'mon, Charles," Tessa said. "Do children really need a full background check? They're kids. What are they going to do—attack me with their bubble gum? We can make an exception this one time."

The guard looked to his colleagues and the soldiers behind him.

"I'm sorry, sir, but that's not going to be possible."

"That's disappointing. I suppose we're all in for a big temper tantrum, then. The kids were really excited about the tour."

Loudmouth stepped forward and shouted something incomprehensible about mean girls and the time saltwater taffy got stuck in her hair. The sound waves were so intense that they knocked the entire group of armed agents and soldiers off their feet.

"See what you've done?" Tessa said to the fallen agents.

Thor pulled the front door of the White House off its hinges and broke it in half over his knee.

Funk raised an armpit and emitted a gaseous green cloud that covered the building's windows, pressing them inward until they shattered. Snot Rocket fired explosive boogers through the doorway. A moment later there was a *KA-POW!* Wood and plaster came flying through the opening.

"Follow me!" Tessa cried, leading her team inside. Miss Information followed proudly. "This is the Green Room, team," Tessa said. "My father uses it to meet with foreign dignitaries. The Queen of England sat on that chair once. He wouldn't let me meet her. What do you think, Loudmouth?"

"Nice place!" Tammy shouted, then turned her voice on the furniture. Antiques splintered, candelabras smashed through windows, and a chandelier worth a million dollars crashed onto a table and showered the room with a billion tiny crystals. An electrical fire ignited where the lamp once hung, filling the room with smoke and setting off a piercing alarm, but none of the BULLIES stayed long enough to be annoyed. There were other rooms to destroy.

"This is my dad's favorite room. They call it the Red Room. He likes to read in here when he should be asking me about my day," Tessa said as she led everyone inside. The scarlet furniture was impeccable. "Funk, you're up!"

The filthy boy laid his hands on the wall and a black mold spread to every corner of the room and every piece of furniture. Soon, mushrooms were growing on chairs and fuzzy white ooze dripped off everything. The air turned sour and putrid, making Miss Information gag.

"I need to show you the best room in the house," Tessa said, rushing out of the Red Room with the rest of the team in tow. She threw open a door and ushered everyone inside. The carpet was a royal blue with the U.S. Great Seal stitched in the center. A large oak desk sat near a bank of windows covered in gold drapes. Several flags stood nearby.

"The Oval Office," Tessa said. "Daddy sits in here and drinks lemonade while he reads national security briefs. I'm not allowed to bother him. He calls it his sanctuary. I hate this room most of all. Tear this place apart!"

Snot Rocket fired a booger at the desk and it exploded. Thor picked up a chair and heaved it through a window. Funk caused a black stain to grow on the ceiling above them. Loudmouth screamed a hole into the wall.

"Brilliant, Tessa!" Miss Information said.

Tessa grinned. "They'll never reelect a guy who let a bunch of kids destroy the world's most famous house."

Miss Information laughed. "He'll be lucky if they don't hang him!"

"You've got to be kidding me," said a voice from behind her. Miss Information turned and looked through the hole that Loudmouth had created in the wall. Five children stood on the lawn. Their leader had poofy blond hair and thick glasses. Next to her was a short African American kid, a heavy-breathing Korean girl, a kid with the worst set of braces she had ever seen, and a jittery kid stuffing orange circus peanuts into his mouth. Seeing them, the pain returned to Miss Information's head. She stumbled, fighting to separate her dream world from the real one.

"We know you sent us to fight your stupid robots at the Hoover Dam," the blond leader said, "but you forgot something very important—we have a rocket."

"Ms. Holiday," the Asian girl said. "We love you very much and we hope we can help you overcome whatever has control over you, but right now you're about to get your butt kicked."

"Who's Ms. Holiday?" Loudmouth shouted.

"Who cares?" Funk asked. "What do we do?"

"Attack!" Tessa said, and the two teams stampeded at each other. Paintings were torn apart, furniture was used as battering rams, punches connected with walls, and several fires broke out. The skinny Mexican kid went toe-to-toe with Thor. The kid with the braces wrestled with Funk. The flying Korean girl buzzed around Loudmouth. Snot Rocket had his hands, and nose, full with the chubby kid who could walk on walls. And Tessa swung a flag stand at the girl with the glasses, who kept breaking out in hives that vanished and reappeared in the blink of an eye.

Miss Information, however, barely noticed the chaos all around her. She was trapped in a slide show of memories so bright and intense they were blinding. She saw a place like the one she had built for her BULLIES; it was called the Playground. There was a man there—a man who made her feel like she was finally home. His name was Alexander, and he was real and she loved him.

She fell over onto the floor, fighting the hallucinations. She needed air, so she ripped off her mask, which only seemed to open the door to a flood of new visions. There was a library at an elementary school, and a little flying globe just like Benjy. There was a yellow rocket and a boy with humongous buck teeth. And

38°53' N, 77°2' W

with each memory there came a peculiar emotion—a mixture of joy and excitement and tenderness. If she hadn't known better, she might have guessed it was love. What was happening to her? She couldn't concentrate and couldn't stand. These kids' arrival had caused her to suffer.

But the mask could protect her. The mask made everything simple. It was her shield and her weapon. It told her who she was. She slipped it back on, and all at once her head was clear. She also knew exactly what she had to do.

"Retreat!" she called. She darted through the hole in the wall and sprinted for the bus. Her team followed, slack-jawed and confused. She dove on board and raced to her seat. Alex was waiting. He had a worried expression on his face. She would explain to him what happened. He would listen.

When the kids tumbled onto the bus, she commanded the lunch lady to drive. But someone was blocking their path—the real president. He peered through the window at his twin, his mouth agape.

"Who are you?" he stammered.

Miss Information smiled. "Show him, Tessa."

Tessa mushed her face back to normal. "It's me," she said, nearly spitting the words at him.

"Tessa?"

"We're done here. Let's go, lunch lady!" Miss Information ordered.

The Antagonist revved the bus's engine and two soldiers dragged President Lipton away. With its path clear, the School Bus ignited its rockets and lifted into the air. Seconds later, it shot into the sky.

"Look, Tessa!" Funk said. "They're arresting your dad."

Tessa looked out the window. Suddenly, her glee changed to something resembling concern, but Miss Information was too busy working out her next scheme to give the girl much thought. She finally knew how to take over the world and destroy her greatest enemies at the same time. She needed to get to work.

14

"Get in here," Sarah said when Ruby finally staggered home from school. "We're in crisis mode."

Ruby took a deep breath. Her mother knew. Of course she knew! Video of the fight had to be on every channel in the world by now. Her whole family probably saw it on the news. Her secret life was over. It was time to come clean.

"Mom, I can explain everything, but you need to listen—"

"Whatever it is, it's going to have to wait," Francis said, rushing into the room with Noah in his arms and Truman following at his heels. "The hotel we booked for the entire family had to close. Their furnace went out and the water pipes froze. They burst and the rooms are flooded. We've called every hotel, motel, YMCA, and youth hostel within a hundred miles, but everyone is booked solid."

Ruby was confused. Hadn't they been watching the news? Hadn't they seen the epic battle at the White House?

"So we have a plan B," Francis said. "Promise you won't freak out."

Ruby couldn't seem to shift gears. "Um—"

"They have to stay here," Sarah said. "With us."

Her mother and father stood cringing as if Ruby were a stick of dynamite with a dwindling fuse. Even Noah and Truman watched with nervous baby eyes and a nervous wagging tail.

"Um, OK. Did you see the news?" Ruby asked.

"Yeah, a little bit. The president went crazy or something. They arrested him. The old folks and the kids have been battling over the TV all day, so unless it was part of a documentary on World War Two or a story involving the Teenage Mutant Ninja Turtles, we didn't hear much about it. Did you hear what we said? The entire family is staying here."

Ruby shook her head to unclog the gunk in her brain. So they didn't know—at least not yet. It was just a matter of time, though. There had been reporters everywhere when the kids were fighting Miss Information and her gang of misfits. Someone had to have gotten a shot of Ruby's face. "Mom, Dad, I need to talk to you about something."

"Sure, what is it honey?" her mother asked.

"In private."

"Yeah, OK," Sarah said. "Let's go to your room."

Ruby tried to think of what to say to her family. How did she start a story as long and as involved as hers? *Mom, Dad, I'm a spy. I have robots in my body. I save the world during school hours. I just got into a fistfight with the president's daughter in the Oval Office.* There was no time to come up with an easy way to tell them about her secret life. It would be a huge shock, but it wasn't fair to—

"WHAT HAPPENED TO MY ROOM?" Ruby cried when she opened her bedroom door.

Every drawer was open. All of her books, pens, clothes, and shoes were scattered on the floor. Board games had been opened and their pieces thrown about like confetti. Her comforter had been used as a makeshift fort, held down by dirty bricks taken from the corner of the garage. A package of cookies had clearly been stepped on and mashed into her carpet, and several juice box containers had leaked onto her pillows. Her neat, super-organized sanctuary smelled of pungent, sweaty children.

"The kids needed a place to play," Sarah explained. "It's no big deal. We'll clean it up."

Suddenly, Ruby's entire body broke out in angry, red welts. Her feet swelled so much that her toes felt like they might burst through her sneakers. Her armpits itched, her nose ran with snot, her ears were clogged and scratchy, and her eyes felt as if someone had rubbed lemons on them. Ruby was allergic to a messy room, but she was even more allergic to being exhausted.

"They ruined everything! You know how I feel about my stuff."

"Ruby, they're your family. You're just going to have to roll with the punches," her mother insisted.

"NO! This house already has two and a half slobs living in it!" she shouted. "Now you want to invite in a hundred more and give them my room? Well, I won't do it! It wasn't my idea to invite everyone here for the holidays, so why should I suffer? These people don't even like each other. They bicker the whole time about which religion slash baseball team slash bagel is the best. They never stop talking, they trash the house, and then they try to guilt us because the two of you apparently aren't raising me and Noah right. I don't know why you had to invite them!"

Ruby heard a slight cough and looked to her right. Her entire extended family was standing in the doorway, listening.

"Someone is getting coal for Christmas," Cousin Finn said.

"Ruby Tallulah Peet!" Sarah cried. "You apologize this minute."

Grandma Tina shook her head. "She's right. We should head home. This is too much for you folks."

"Mom, don't you dare take a step toward that door," Sarah said. "You are more than welcome here."

"Ruby, I think you need to spend a little time in your room

ATTACK OF THE BULLIES

thinking about being rude to the people who love you," Francis said as he slammed shut her bedroom door.

Ruby scooted the juice boxes off her pillow and threw herself onto her bed. She lay on her back, staring at the ceiling, bewildered by what she had just done. Sure, there were going to be something like fifty thousand people sleeping in her home that night, but why get so angry? Normally, she would have been thrilled with the chance to find a truckload of inflatable mattresses and quilts. She could have happily taken over the whole operation. So, why wasn't she?

Was it really about her family's bickering and the kids going through her sock drawers? No, she knew it wasn't. Her messy room was just a reflection of her messy life. It felt like one layer of trouble was stacked on top of another, and then another, like a birthday cake of chaos.

And she had taken all of it out on her family. She needed to apologize.

She got up from her bed, ready to throw herself at the mercy of the entire Peet/Kaplan clan, when she heard a message alert coming from the computer in her backpack. She popped it open and found an encrypted e-mail from Duncan. She ran the decryption program and found a link to a video on a news website. A reporter stood in front of the busted fence outside the White House.

"Folks, this isn't some big-budget Hollywood movie," he

said. "Superheroes are real. I'm here at 1600 Pennsylvania Avenue, the scene of a battle right out of a comic book. As we reported earlier, President Lipton was arrested for leading an assault on the White House. Rumors circulated that he was with a group of superpowered children. We can now confirm that those rumors are true. We've got footage of the event, and I assure you, this is the real thing."

The reporter vanished and a video of the fight replaced him. Ruby's heart sank, fully expecting to recognize her face or those of her teammates.

"As you can see, one of these so-called superkids can fly. The other seems to be able to create things with the braces on his teeth. Now here's one who appears to be able to create sonic booms with her voice. But most shocking of all is an exclusive image of President Lipton commanding a boy to fire what appears to be exploding mucus at Secret Service agents."

Ruby watched intently. She saw Flinch leaping into the air and Duncan spraying glue out of his fingers and her own poofy hair as she fought Tessa Lipton disguised as the president, but the camera was shaky. There wasn't a steady shot of anyone's face. Could they really have been so lucky?

The reporter's voice returned. "As we've reported, there is no information on what prompted the president's actions or where these superpowered children came from. We've been told that President Lipton is in custody at the Pentagon. Sources say he is refusing to cooperate with the CIA and the FBI. At the moment, we have no comment from the White House or from the First Lady, but it is assumed that Vice President James Stephenson will be sworn in as soon as possible."

The video switched to a wrinkly old man with an angry face. He wore a suit and stood at a podium in front of a room of reporters.

"The Senate majority leader had this to say about the incident," the reporter said.

"When I was a kid if we wanted to go somewhere we walked! Now the sky is overrun with flying children. Clearly, the president is behind this. Perhaps he was some kind of sleeper agent. These kids could be Russians, North Koreans, or even aliens from another planet. But I believe this wild act of violence and these superpowered children are a direct result of playing too many video games. With the beeps and the boops and the cranky birds. It rots their brains. I think the good people of this country are starting to realize that video games are the cause of all the world's problems—that and rock music."

Ruby closed her laptop and sighed. It was a miracle that the NERDS had not been identified. Maybe her life wasn't falling apart after all.

Suddenly, her scalp began to itch. She leaped from her seat

and swung her leg around, connecting with the man that stood next to her bed. She clipped his chin and he fell backward, knocking over a lamp.

"I'm allergic to being snuck up on," Ruby said. "I'm also allergic to strangers crawling in through my bedroom window, creepy grown-ups, and being underestimated."

"Are you Ruby Peet?" the man asked as he staggered to his feet.

Ruby leaped forward with fists clenched. She threw several

punches, connecting with the man's jaw and sending him into a shelf that held her trophies for Best Gift Wrapping.

The man was well trained. He threw his own punches, aiming for her chest and gut. She tumbled into her desk, knocking a piggy bank to the floor and shattering it. Change rolled all over the floor. That hurt—a lot. She knew if she didn't want to feel another hit, she needed to calm down and let her allergies tell her what to do.

Her tongue was swollen, which meant he was about to

deliver a knee to her face. She blocked it and kicked his other leg out from under him. A pronounced wheeze in her lungs meant he was going to put her in a bear hug, but she squirmed out of the way and clunked him on the head with her computer. A weepy eye told her that she needed to step to the right to avoid an uppercut. The man swung with all his strength, throwing himself off-balance. He slammed onto the floor with a thud and Ruby leaped on top of him, twisting his arm into a chicken wing.

"If you want to keep throwing that tantrum, you should be prepared to be grounded for two weeks, young lady!" her father shouted through her closed door.

"If you want to keep getting beat up, you're going to have to do it more quietly," Ruby hissed at her attacker.

"Kid, I'm not here to fight you. I work for the Secret Service. I know who you are. I know who you work for."

"Who sent you?"

"General Savage."

Ruby snarled.

"He just wants to have a conversation."

"The general?"

"No, the president. Can you let me up?"

"The president doesn't have security clearance high enough to talk to me," Ruby said. "Besides, isn't he in jail?"

"Yes, an innocent man has been arrested, and you're involved. The very least you could do is go talk to him, kid."

Deep within the Pentagon, the president sat in a bare room. His hands were cuffed together and he looked exhausted.

"So it's true," he said when Ruby sat down in front of him.

She frowned. "What's true, sir?"

"This country has a spy organization made up of superpowered children," he said. There was a manila folder on the table with the words TOP SECRET printed on it. He pushed it toward her, but she didn't open it. She already knew what was in it and who had given it to him.

"Let's talk about your daughter, sir."

"Is she one of you?"

Ruby shook her head. "No, but she's being led by someone who used to be a member of our team."

The principal opened his folder and peered at a document inside. "Yes, the librarian—Viktoriya Deprankova."

"We prefer to call her Ms. Holiday."

"She's now calling herself Miss Information, right?"

"I can't tell you anything, sir."

"I'm the president, young lady."

"I understand. But you're not my boss," she said.

The president growled. "Then tell Tessa's father. That was her today, right?"

Ruby nodded. She had seen his daughter's transformation herself. Tessa could change her appearance at will. Miss Information appeared to have built her own upgrade chair and filled her BULLIES full of nanobytes.

"Does it have to do with that virus? The one that made everybody criminals?"

Ruby shook her head. "I can't be certain that Tessa is not under the influence of something, but it's not the virus. I want you to know that we're working hard to find her and stop her—"

"Good. I've directed the CIA to take command of the search," the president interrupted. "They'll be joining you in your headquarters—the one you call the Playground. I understand you have an incredible amount of technology at your disposal. We'll need it to find my daughter and stop that madwoman. You and the other kids will support their efforts. General Savage has agreed to come in and head up the mission. I think that will work well since you already have a working relationship with him."

Ruby swallowed hard. "And when it's all over and Tessa is safe and sound, what happens to us?"

The president blinked. "You?"

"Yes, what happens to NERDS? Will the CIA go away and let us do our work in peace?"

"We'll cross that bridge when we get to it, young lady," the president said as two men in lab coats entered the room. One was holding a hypodermic needle. "In the meantime these doctors need a little blood test. I'm sure you don't mind."

Suddenly, Ruby let out a huge sneeze.

"Ruby, I'm going to get you out of there."

She had never been so happy to hear Heathcliff's voice.

All of a sudden, the lights went out, and she sprang to her feet and darted into the dark hallway, with confused and angry guards in hot pursuit. Ruby was allergic to slamming face-first into walls, so she didn't have to slow down as Heathcliff fed her turn-for-turn directions. Finally, she pushed a fire exit door open and ran into the night. The principal was in his Jeep, waiting for her by the side of the road.

"They know about us," Ruby said.

The principal nodded. "I know."

"What do we do?"

"We do what Brand told us to do. We destroy the Playground."

15

Heathcliff Hodges collected his few possessions: a pair of sneakers, some clothes, a stack of notebooks, a framed photo of his parents, and the assorted parts of Benjamin. He tossed them into a backpack just as the door flew open.

"Grab your things," Jackson Jones shouted. "We've lost our lease! Everything must go! Take whatever isn't nailed down and meet the team in the control center."

Heathcliff veered toward the science room. He found Duncan racing from one table to the next, snatching things and shoving them into two huge duffel bags.

"We should take the jet packs," Heathcliff said.

Duncan nodded. "I took three. That's as much as I could

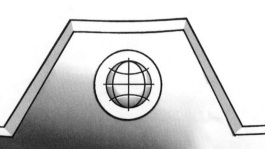

carry. There's some exploding bubble gum back there that could be useful."

"Actually, I was hoping I might find the potion they wanted to use on my parents."

Duncan frowned. "I don't know. I never met the team assigned to it. It could be anywhere."

Heathcliff stared out at the hundred workstations.

"Attention, all personnel." An amplified voice echoed through the Playground. "This is the principal. The Playground has been compromised. Agents of the federal government are on their way. I'm activating Directive 86 right now. You have two minutes to leave or you're staying forever. This is not a test. I repeat, this is not a test."

Red lights flashed and a loud warning siren blared. Heathcliff raced from table to table. He needed the cure for his parents so that they would remember him, but it was like searching for a four-leaf clover—only the clover patch was going to explode in two minutes.

Flinch appeared, desperately trying to close a suitcase overflowing with candy. "C'mon, we need to get out of here."

"I have to find the potion," Heathcliff shouted.

Matilda joined them, dragging her favorite combat dummy behind her.

"You two need to get to the control room," she yelled.

"I can't go until I find it!"

The principal and Ruby zoomed into the Playground together.

"Let's go," the principal said. "I won't let them ruin what we've built here. You kids are too valuable to the world."

Heathcliff continued to search frantically. "Who was working on the potion?"

"Son, get in the control room *now*," the principal said.

"I won't go!" Heathcliff cried.

There was a sound like a giant redwood tree splintering and crashing to the forest floor and a thick gray liquid began to fill the room.

"What's that?" he asked.

"Concrete," the principal said. "We're burying it alive. If anyone ever stumbles upon this facility, it will be completely useless to them. Heathcliff, I'm only going to say this one more time."

Didn't they understand? He needed that potion. "Go on without me."

"Matilda, does that inhaler of yours have a tranquilizer in it?"

Matilda nodded and aimed her inhaler at Heathcliff.

"Don't do this!" he begged.

"Sorry," she said.

There was a loud pop and a sting on the side of his neck, and all the fight in him melted away.

Flinch hefted Heathcliff onto his back and all of the NERDS raced to the control room.

The principal pushed a button and the floor began to rise, though Heathcliff couldn't be sure it wasn't the tranquilizer that was making him feel floaty. He watched as the secret headquarters for the National Espionage, Rescue, and Defense Society vanished below him. There were several loud explosions, and then the lights went out.

"So we're homeless?" Duncan asked.

"What about the elementary school?" Ruby asked. "Can't we go back to that one?"

The principal shook his head. "Directive 86 shuts down the middle school, the elementary school, and the high school all at the same time."

"So that's it? That's the end?" Matilda said.

"No, it's not the end," the principal replied. "We're just moving to the backup facility."

"What backup facility?" Flinch said.

That was the last thing Heathcliff heard before he lost consciousness.

END TRANSMISSION.

TOP SECRET DOSSIER

CODE NAME: SICKBED
REAL NAME: MARVIN TAYLOR
YEARS ACTIVE: 1981-83
CURRENT OCCUPATION:
PROFESSIONAL MEDICAL
TEST SUBJECT

HISTORY: MARVIN SPENT MOST OF HIS YOUNG LIFE IN BED, SICK WITH A COLD, FEVER, FLU, SORE THROAT, MIGRAINE HEADACHE, OR CHICKEN POX. IF ANYONE WAS SICK WITHIN A FIFTY-MILE RADIUS, IT WAS ALMOST GUARANTEED THAT AGENT SICKBED WOULD CATCH IT. HE WAS THE ONLY AGENT IN NERDS HISTORY WHO ASKED TO BE PAID IN KLEENEX. HE WAS ALSO THE ONLY AGENT OFFICIALLY EXEMPT FROM FILING REPORTS; THE TEAM'S DIRECTOR SAID HE COULDN'T READ WHAT MARVIN WROTE DUE TO THE SNOT AND BOOGERS ON EVERY PAGE.

UPGRADE: SICKBED COULD GIVE
AN ENEMY GERMS AND VIRUSES AT
WILL, CAUSING THEM TO FALL ILL
WITHIN SECONDS, ALL FROM
A SINGLE COUGH.

LEVEL 6
ACCESS GRANTED

BEGIN TRANSMISSION:

16

Tessa's father had been arrested
and it was her fault. Unlike that morning, when her anger at
him was something bitter in her mouth she wanted to spit
onto the floor, she felt nothing but despair. She'd gone too
far. She just wanted him to lose the election, not wind up in
prison. What if he went to jail for the rest of his life? How
would she live with herself?

"So are you going to step aside or not?" Funk demanded.

"Huh?" Tessa said, startled by his anger.

The rest of the BULLIES surrounded her.

"You're not smart enough or tough enough to lead this
team!" Snot Rocket shouted. "Plus, your upgrade is L-A-M-E.
If anyone should be running this group, it's me. I have the
most experience. I've spent the last three years in in-school

suspension. I've been in twenty fistfights this month, and eighty percent were with teachers."

"Unfortunately, you didn't win any of them," Funk snarled, then turned his rage on Tessa. "I should be in charge. I'm the coolest one under pressure. When that kid was pouring that sticky gunk on me, I didn't even flinch."

"Which is why you're still completely trapped in it," Loudmouth cried. "A leader has to command respect, and no one can command like me. I don't want to lead this team, but to be honest, I don't see any other solution."

Thor grunted. No one could understand a word he said, but Tessa knew what he meant. He wanted to be in charge, too.

Normally, Tessa would have bristled at a challenge to her dominance. At Sugarland, no one would have dared to get in her face, but after the day's events she didn't care anymore. Any one of them could be the leader of this stupid team. "Fine. I quit."

"Tessa!" Miss Information called when she entered the room. She had her straw boyfriend in her arms and madness in her eyes, and she was waving her finger back and forth in a *don't even think about it* gesture.

Tessa had a sudden vision of her future, and it involved tigers with overstuffed bellies licking their greasy chops. At that moment she would've been happy to have bugs splattering on her face if it meant she could fly away and escape.

"You're not going anywhere," Miss Information continued.

Tessa shook her head. "This isn't what I signed up for. I didn't think my dad would be arrested."

"Really? You pretended to be him and then trashed the home of the most powerful person on the planet. What did you think was going to happen?"

"I just wanted him to lose the election so he would have more time for me."

"Tessa, that's what will happen! When you go see him during the prison's visiting hours, you'll have his undivided attention. It will be through a Plexiglass window—but he will be all yours."

"I'm going to turn myself in to the police. I can't let him be imprisoned for something I did."

"Oh, honey, you know I can't let you do that," her boss said with more than a hint of menace. "You kids are so spoiled these days. I just don't know what will make you happy. I suppose I have to fix your problem again."

"Fix it? How? Do you mean break him out of jail?"

Miss Information sighed. "We could, but then you and your family would live like fugitives, sleeping in abandoned buildings and eating rats and discarded banana peels. I'm sure you'd give me the boo-boo face for that, too."

"Then what are you talking about?"

"We have to make it so that today never happened at all."

As Tessa searched the room for exits, a copper-skinned woman with eyeglasses and a white lab coat stepped into the command center. She looked exhausted, hungry, and in desperate need of a shower. She trembled when Miss Information turned to her.

"Ma'am, I have some very good news," she said, her voice squeaking. "We cracked the problem with your latest design. We're testing it as we speak."

"See! I told you if you just followed my drawings it would be easy to build," Miss Information said proudly.

"Ma'am, you drew a picture of an old DeLorean sports car with the words *Time Machine* at the bottom," the scientist said.

Miss Information turned to her scarecrow boyfriend. "Isn't this just grand, darling! It's the final piece of my master plan. Oh, yes, you're right. There *is* a lot of work to do, and not a minute to spare. Well, actually, now that we have a time machine, we have all the minutes we want. But I'm eager to get started."

She gave the scarecrow a passionate kiss on his painted mouth.

The BULLIES pretended not to notice.

"Where's my Benjy?" she asked.

The little silver orb floated into the room. "I am here."

"Benjy, have you studied the footage of our attack on the White House?"

"I have."

"So you noticed the five children who gave the BULLIES a resounding kick in the pants?"

"I did. I saw the pants-kicking."

"I want you to find as much information as you can about them and their families, going back several generations."

"I will start at once," Benjy said, and zipped out of the room.

"Oh, this is going to be so much fun. I don't know why I didn't think of it before."

"Think of what?" Funk asked.

"Erasing my enemies. I have a feeling it will cure those pesky headaches, too."

"Can you please tell me what is going on?" Tessa asked.

Miss Information squeezed her arm so tight it hurt. "Tessa, you and the rest of the BULLIES are going to accompany Benjy, Alex, and me into the past, where we will locate the ancestors of the kids who attacked you today. Then we will make sure that our mutual enemies were never born. The world will be mine, and there will be a nice side effect for you—today will have never happened. Without the NERDS, there would be no reason for me to have recruited you, given you superpowers, and taken you to the White House to ruin your dad's life. All the trouble will vanish in an instant. Plus, since I will be running everything when we get back, your dad will be out of a job.

You'll get everything I promised you, Tessa. Everything! Are you in?"

Miss Information was crazy. But Tessa had just seen impossible things: kids who could fly, snot that exploded, stink that could level a house, and her own malleable face. When Miss Information said she could go back in time, Tessa believed it. Her plan might be the only thing Tessa could do to save her father.

She nodded. "I'm in."

Miss Information turned to the rest of the team. "Each one of you has a valuable skill. Tessa's is leadership, and I want her in charge. If you have a problem with that, I have a couple starving tigers I'd like you to meet. Any questions?"

The BULLIES frowned but said nothing.

"Hooray!" she cried. "I'm glad everyone is happy. Let's go back in time!"

17

"This is the backup facility for an international spy organization?" Ruby asked, staring up at the sign for Marty Mozzarella's restaurant. The brightly colored logo was a big, grinning mouse wearing a Rastafarian hat.

"It is," the principal said.

Ruby was speechless. Marty Mozzarella's was a restaurant for little kids. The food was a crime against humanity: The pizza tasted like an old man's slipper dipped in ketchup, the french fries were as soggy as a rag at a car wash, and the chicken fingers might well have been made from the fingers of an actual chicken. Plus, next to the tables, there were fifty decibel-busting video games that shook the air with blinks, bonks, beeps, and blasts.

"My dad brought me here for pizza and games once when

I was little. It was fun until he found a dirty diaper in the ball pit," Duncan said. "I haven't been back since."

Matilda gagged.

"Note to self: Do not eat in this restaurant," Jackson said.

Flinch shrugged. "Speak for yourself. This place has the best food ever."

Heathcliff didn't care where they were headquartered. On the ride from the Playground he had switched back and forth from tears to bitterness. Ruby understood why he was so mad, but she had bigger problems on her hands than wiping tears off the face of former agent Choppers. Aside from having to run for her life from the president of the United States and being exposed as a spy, she had disappeared from her parents' house, after shouting that she hated all her relatives. They must have discovered she was missing by now. Her whole family would be in a panic.

Once inside the dingy restaurant, Ruby's allergies went haywire. Her lips swelled up, her fingers got puffy, and her ears ached. Her eyes watered like faucets and her swelling ankles threatened to split her sneakers. One look around explained why. She was in a restaurant filled with a mob of sticky-faced pre-kindergartners who wiped their runny noses on their hands and then wiped their hands on anything that didn't move. But it was the actual employees that made her suffer the most. She was allergic to minimum-wage, dead-end jobs and hopelessness. She reached into her pocket for an allergy tablet and swallowed it dry.

Most of the team squeezed into a booth with the principal while Flinch, mesmerized by the lights and sounds, decided to have a look around.

"So, as you can tell, we've got a few problems," the principal said, trying to shout over a robotic Marty and his vermin friends singing the Happy Birthday song to a screaming kid.

"What about our parents?" Jackson asked.

"Yeah, they're going to be worried when we don't come home," Matilda said.

"And what are we going to do to protect them? I'm sure the Secret Service will want to question them. What if they're taken into custody to try to force us out?" Duncan asked.

"Most of your parents are aware of your secret lives. I contacted everyone's except for Heathcliff's and Ruby's."

Heathcliff groaned, then got up and stomped off.

"I should go see them," Ruby said.

"I think that is a terrible idea," the principal said. "Going home will put them in danger. The Secret Service will be watching your house, and the second you show up they'll have you. Right now, the best thing you can do is let your parents believe you ran away."

Ruby was shocked by his idea. "You want to make them worry?"

"Your parents will call the cops and report you missing and the police will show up and do an investigation. With police in the house, the Secret Service and the CIA might keep their distance. All those cops and all those family members might buy us a little time until we can finish this mission. Ruby, I know you hate this idea, but it's the best one we've got right now."

A teenager in a mouse costume approached their booth.

"Excuse me, but is he with you?" he asked, pointing toward a candy machine. Inside were mounds of chocolates and sweets with a large mechanical claw above them. Flinch had his arm trapped inside the dispenser, yet he was singing with joy. "He's scaring the other kids."

"Oh, but the six-foot rat bringing them food isn't freaking them out?" Jackson asked.

"Hey, don't say 'rat' in here. I'm a mouse! Do you want the health department coming down on us?"

Duncan stood up. "I'll go get him."

"Thank you," the mouse said as he rushed off to take an order.

Jackson's braces whirred nervously. "Is this place safe? If they find us, it's only a matter of time before we're lab rats."

"Hey, kid!" the man in the mouse suit shouted from across the room. "Shut it!"

"Sorry," Jackson said sheepishly.

The principal shook his head. "This restaurant is completely off the grid," he said. "Only myself, Agent Brand, and a few former directors even know it exists. Best of all, soon it will be completely operational. We'll have the full science team here before long."

Ruby looked around the restaurant. She hadn't noticed at first, but most of the cooks were scientists from the Playground. Now, instead of lab coats, they were wearing T-shirts with MARTY MOZZARELLA on the front and sliding trays of garlic knots into the ovens.

Duncan returned with Flinch, who was carrying a droopy slice of pepperoni and mushroom. "This place rules!"

Ruby turned to the principal. "What are we supposed to do in this dump?"

"This 'dump' is filled with massive computing power," the principal said. He squeezed out of the booth, crossed the room, and pressed his hand on a game's screen. A green light scanned his fingertips and then the game disappeared, replaced by an array of surveillance camera images from all over the world. "Every one of these arcade games has a hard drive with processor speeds far beyond anything we had at the Playground. The kitchen is stocked with the latest weaponry. There are surface-to-air missiles inside that robot squirrel over there."

"So what's the plan?" Matilda asked.

"The same as it was yesterday: Find Tessa Lipton. Only this time we're not rescuing her. We're bringing her to justice."

"One suggestion!" Flinch cried, his mouth full of pizza. "Can we make this place our permanent headquarters? It's amazing and the food is yum!"

38° 46' N, 77° 4' W

"That looks like a Sit 'n Spin," Funk snarled.

Tessa had to agree. Miss Information's time machine appeared to be a very large version of a toy that caused her to throw up all over herself when she was four years old. *Oh, what a delightful present that was,* she thought. *Hours of gut-wrenching fun!*

"Are you sure you didn't just swipe that from a playground?" Snot Rocket asked.

"We tried several designs, but this one promised to be the safest for the passengers," the tired scientist replied. Tessa had learned her name was Dr. Rajkumar and that she was an expert on temporal physics—whatever that was.

"Why does it need to be safe?" Tammy screamed.

"Because it rips a hole in the fabric of time and space," Dr. Rajkumar said. "To create the anomaly necessary for time travel, the machine has to generate power on the levels comparable to a supernova and—"

"Blah, blah, blah, science!" interrupted Miss Information. "So . . . how do we use it?"

"The passenger enters the precise date, time, longitude, and latitude into the control pad, then turns the wheel. A wormhole will open and everyone on board will be pulled through it. When your mission is complete, just press the HOME button and it will bring you back here."

"Easy breezy," Miss Information said.

"But at great personal risk to my health and well-being, I have to insist that you not do this," Dr. Rajkumar said.

"PREPARE THE TIGERS!" Miss Information yelled.

"Please, I beg you. What you want to do could have very nasty side effects. If you go into the past and change something, there is no way of predicting the ripple effect it will have on the present. Let's say you cause an accident that kills someone—hypothetically, say the grandfather of Alexander Fleming—"

"Who?" Tessa asked.

"The man who discovered penicillin. What if you accidently killed his grandfather? Hundreds of thousands—

maybe even millions—of people would be dead because he never invented the vaccine."

"Attention, kids, do not kill Alexander Fleming . . . OK—anything else?"

"Yes! Changes aren't always so straightforward. Any little thing could change the course of human history. The simplest action could literally destroy the world—stepping on an ant, causing a traffic accident, stealing someone's parking spot—all of these things could be tied to much bigger, much more important events. Cutting someone off in traffic could literally be tied to the birth of another human being. There's just no way of knowing."

"Consider us warned," Miss Information said. "Now, let's give my new toy a spin. Benjy, have you compiled that list I asked you for?"

"I have," the robot said as it zipped into the room. "On August 16, 1987, Edgar Escala—Julio Escala's grandfather—visited Washington, D.C., on vacation from Mexico City and made a stop at an immigration office to get information on becoming a United States citizen. Public records show that Edgar signed in at the visitors' center at 8:05 A.M. on the date in question. There is a ninety-seven percent chance that this experience directly lead to Mr. Escala moving his family to the United States."

"Well, we're going to have to find a way to change his mind," Miss Information said as she stepped onto the time machine's platform.

"I'm downloading the information, time, and coordinates into your machine as well as all the information I collected about the other NERDS and their families," Benjy chirped.

Dr. Rajkumar blanched. "This is your plan? Making sure those kids were never born?"

"You got it! Kids, let's go," Miss Information said, dismissing the scientist and ushering Tessa and the others onto the Sit 'n Spin platform. Tessa didn't like the idea of erasing someone, but she couldn't leave her father in jail. She and the others turned the big wheel at the center of the machine, and it started to spin.

"I don't feel so good," Snot Rocket said as the wheel spun faster and faster.

"Yeah, I'm not sure about this," Tammy cried as the air grew very cold and crackled with electricity.

Tessa felt very nauseous herself, and it wasn't just from the spinning. The machine was making her insides feel like a bottle of soda shaken by a mischievous child. She was sure she was going to pop.

"I want to get off," Funk whined. "We have to stop this!"

But Miss Information ignored his plea and the wheel

turned even faster. The underground lair vanished and a series of images of people and places appeared: a woman slapped a man in a nightclub, a teenager danced at a rock concert, a little boy played kickball, a dog pulled his owner down the street, a soldier hurried across a war-torn lanscape, a man and a woman got married with a little white dog at their feet. They seemed to come from all different time periods. Could the rest of the team see them, too?

And then Tessa saw her father creeping into her bedroom at

the White House, sitting down next to her, and watching her sleep.

"Dad?"

There was a final flash and he vanished along with the other visions, and Tessa was startled to find that she and her team were no longer in Miss Information's secret lair. Somehow they were in the middle of a busy Washington, D.C., street, and there was a bus barreling right at them.

TOP SECRET DOSSIER

CODE NAME: PIZZA FACE
REAL NAME: DENISE BERNAKE
YEARS ACTIVE: 1984-88
CURRENT OCCUPATION:
ROCKET SCIENTIST

HISTORY: DENISE WAS ONE OF THOSE POOR CHILDREN WHO SUFFER FROM EARLY-ONSET PUBERTY. ONE DAY SHE WAS A SMILING, SWEET LITTLE GIRL AND THE NEXT SHE HAD A FACE FULL OF ZITS. NO AMOUNT OF ACNE MEDICINE SEEMED TO HAVE ANY EFFECT, BUT HER SAD AFFLICTION WAS TURNED INTO A TREMENDOUS ASSET WITH THE HELP OF MODERN TECHNOLOGY.

UPGRADE: USE YOUR IMAGINATION, KID. WHAT COULD A GIRL WITH A FACE FULL OF ERUPTING PIMPLES DO? JUST THINKING ABOUT WRITING IT DOWN MAKES ME GAG.

LEVEL 7
ACCESS GRANTED

BEGIN TRANSMISSION:

19

38°50' N, 77°3' W

Heathcliff needed to take his mind off his parents and his heartbreak, so he decided to turn his attention to the other dilemma—namely, filling in the holes of his Swiss cheese memory. He was convinced that Benjamin was the key to unlocking the mystery, so he worked with a feverish passion, replacing each tiny chip and wire while the rest of the team had one of their stupid secret meetings in a booth at Marty Mozzarella's.

He sat in a dark corner of the restaurant and tested circuits and installed a new cooling system. Then he worked on Benjamin's gyroscopic flight simulator, which gave the robot its ability to fly. Finally, he snapped the ball shut. There were still functions to reconnect and tests to administer, but surely none of them were vital to Benjamin's operation. He pushed

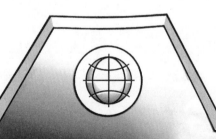

the button on the side of the orb and listened as it hummed to life. A bright red light glowed inside, a signal that there was a serious internal error, but then the light changed to Benjamin's familiar blue, followed by some loud clicking and beeping and then finally . . .

"Heathcliff?"

"Benjamin! Boy, am I glad to hear your voice. You were damaged, but I repaired you, and I've got a million questions."

"Ms. Holiday is—"

Benjamin's blue light turned red and there was a loud POP! Black smoke seeped through the casing, and the ball fell to the floor.

Heathcliff cried out. How could he have been so stupid? His eagerness to know the truth had gotten the best of him, and now he'd probably made Benjamin worse. He picked up the robot and gingerly opened the cover. Much of the circuitry he had installed was melted.

"Any luck?" Jackson asked. The boy stood a few feet away, watching Heathcliff curiously.

Heathcliff grunted. He might have been lonely, but he wasn't about to get chummy with his archenemy. A million atomic wedgies flashed in his memory.

"That's great. We could use Benjamin's help. And we could use yours, too," Jackson said.

Heathcliff wanted to tell him to jump off a bridge. He wanted to laugh in his face. He wanted to spit at him. How dare Jackson come to him for help when he and the others shunned him every day? Oh, the indignity! He felt the rage coursing through every vein, and in that anger was something familiar, something comfortable—like a pair of fluffy socks or his stuffed penguin. That anger would protect him from heartbreak and humiliation.

"Unless you still need a little time on your own," Jackson said.

Heathcliff blinked. "You think I *want* to be alone?"

Jackson shrugged. "To be honest, I wasn't sure how you felt. I know how I would feel if my dad didn't remember me and the only thing that would fix him was buried in cement. I'd want to be alone for a while. And then I'd want a friend."

"You want to be my friend?" Heathcliff asked.

Jackson nodded. "When you're ready. I know I have a lot to make up for."

Heathcliff felt the anger drain out of him like water in a spaghetti strainer. He wasn't ready to throw his arms around Jackson and forgive him, but his armor of hate felt claustrophobic.

"Listen, I know you're bummed about that formula, but the scientist who was working on it wasn't buried in the Playground.

He's here somewhere, probably making breadsticks or cleaning the grease traps. He can start over. That's the cool thing about life. If you want, you can start all over. So, can you give us a hand or should I call you a whaa-mbulance?"

Heathcliff smiled. "Lead the way."

It was late, and the restaurant was closed. The team members were busy working on the various arcade games scattered about the room. Flinch was completely hypnotized by a game called Dig Dug, while Matilda was at a game called Donkey Kong.

"Glad you could join us," the principal told Heathcliff as he stuffed a fistful of gold tokens into his hand.

Heathcliff found a console called Joust that appeared to be a nonsensical game where knights rode flying ostriches over a river of lava. He sank a coin into the slot and a green light appeared on the screen. Instinctively, he placed his hand on it.

The game vanished, replaced by a list of the computer's applications. He scanned the list line by line. The game had the most advanced Web-browsing program he had ever seen. He could read through classified materials from the CIA, the FBI, the IRS, and something called Project Blue Book. He could use facial recognition technology, every satellite circling the world, the Hubble Space Telescope, and the onboard computers of the International Space Station. The list went on and on, and for the first time since he had awakened without his memories he felt like a spy—a real spy!

"What's our priority?" Heathcliff asked.

"We have to find Miss Information," Ruby said. "She's within a hundred miles of the White House."

"How do you know that?"

"I did some calculations on that flying bus of hers. A machine that size and shape could only hold so much fuel. They could get about five hundred miles out of it, assuming it flies as fast as a passenger plane."

"They flew west, too. I've been searching satellites for an appropriate landing site," Duncan said.

"There's an easier way to track them," Heathcliff said. He called them over to his game, where he'd accessed a government weather-tracking site. "We can track their exhaust. The fumes left behind will stay in the air for at least a day afterward."

He showed them a satellite image of Washington, D.C., at the time of the attack, then ran it through a pollution filter until a green band crossed from one side of the screen to the other.

"Like a trail of bread crumbs," he said. "We need a higher-res picture, but once I get that, this will tell us exactly where the ship went."

The principal nodded. "That's good work, Hodges. Keep us in the loop."

Heathcliff's proud grin felt like it was stretching his face so wide it might not return to normal.

"If you find her, we can go home," Duncan said.

"Who wants to go home?" Flinch cried while munching on cold pizza.

"I'll automate the search. If we're lucky, we might have an address by tomorrow morning," Heathcliff said. "What else can I do?"

The principal smiled. "You can help Ruby with surveillance. Miss Information and Tessa must have been captured on video somewhere. It might help us narrow down their location faster."

"And what are *you* going to do, boss?" Matilda said.

"I'm going to make some calls. You and your families are going to need new identities. I have friends in the FBI who will do me some favors."

Heathcliff took a chair and sat next to Ruby, who was busy on a Ms. Pac-Man machine. "Thanks," he said.

Ruby cringed. "For?"

"Letting me help. Most of the time you guys won't even look at me. Nice to know I'm not invisible."

"You're not invisible," Ruby said.

"Are you OK? You look worried."

"I've decided not to tell my parents where I am. It's going to hurt them a lot, but it's going to keep them safe, too. I feel terrible," she said as she flipped through several screens of footage.

"I'm sorry," Heathcliff said. "Families are important, and it's hard when you can't protect them. Especially from something you're responsible for."

Ruby looked at him suspiciously. "Jackson told you what you did?"

He shook his head. "No, but I know it was something bad."

He silently prayed that she would deny it, but she didn't. Instead, she turned her attention back to the screen.

"Are you monitoring wiretaps, too—you know, cell phone chatter?"

"Yes, and I haven't heard a peep," she said. "But I suspect Ms. Holiday's too smart to use a phone."

"You're probably right," Heathcliff said. There were so many cameras to monitor. It was like trying to find a specific seashell on a beach. "I can make an adjustment that will make all of this much easier."

Ruby stepped back and let him work. Heathcliff pushed buttons so furiously the game rattled. Being a part of the team again gave him a joy and excitement that made him feel like a pot boiling over with water. When he was finished, the screen had three images on it: Ms. Holiday, with and without the mask, and Tessa Lipton.

"This surveillance program has facial recognition, but it's sort of lame."

"It's state-of-the-art," Ruby objected.

"I'd hardly call what it does 'art.' It takes six facial features and tries to pinpoint them from grainy video. I'm stunned it *ever* works. I increased its parameters and now it's searching for one hundred fifteen thousand different elements, as well as vocal cues. I'm accessing Ms. Holiday's employee files so we can add in her favorite foods, authors, television shows, actors, whatever. We can link these things to the search and cross-reference receipts from every purchase in the world. Getting more detailed actually makes it simpler. Tessa Lipton is even easier. She's famous. Sooner or later they are going to be seen. They're girls."

"So?"

"Girls like to shop."

"That's sort of offensive," Ruby grumbled. "And not true! Not every girl in the world likes to shop."

"Not every girl. But those two? Absolutely. Ms. Holiday never wore a cardigan twice, and from what I've read, Tessa has a thing for high-end fashion," Heathcliff said.

"You've read that Tessa Lipton likes fashion? Where?"

"In *People* magazine."

"When do you read *People* magazine?"

"I've been locked up without much to do for three months. I'd read *Ladies' Home Journal* if you gave me a copy. There are a few other things we can add to the search, too," Heathcliff continued as he jammed the joystick back and forth. "Why just video? We can add newspapers, magazines, and social media sites. Our targets could appear in the background of someone else's photos and this 'state-of-the-art' program wouldn't catch it."

"I think you're going a bit overboard," Ruby said, nudging the boy aside. He could tell he was making her uncomfortable. She still didn't trust him.

Suddenly, there was an alert and an image appeared on the screen.

"We've got a hit!" Ruby said.

It was a black-and-white newspaper photograph of a car crash on a street across town. In the background, they could see Ms. Holiday in her mask, along with Tessa and the rest of the kids who had attacked them the day before.

"They caused some kind of accident," Heathcliff said. "But wait—this can't be right. This newspaper article is decades old."

Ruby glanced at the newspaper's masthead. It was published August 16, 1987—more than twenty-five years ago.

"I don't understand. The hard drive should have no problems with this," Heathcliff said defensively.

"Well, whatever you did is making it screwy," Ruby said. "Is this one of your schemes?"

"Schemes?" Heathcliff said.

Ruby eyed him closely. "Never mind," she said as she jumped up from her chair. "I need something to eat."

Heathcliff's heart sank. *So much for being a member of the team.*

20

38°53' N, 77°1' W

If it weren't for Loudmouth, the
BULLIES' trip through time would have been cut very short
and had an extremely painful ending. When they were jerked
out of the time stream, they found themselves in the middle of
the street with a bus barreling down on them. Tammy huffed
and puffed, ranting about boys not liking girls with glasses
and overdue library books. Her voice slammed into the bus,
bringing it to a violent stop.

But the BULLIES were not out of danger yet. A car careened
out of the bus lane and headed straight at them. Snot Rocket
fired an explosive booger at the ground, which created a pothole.
The car drove into it headfirst.

A siren wailed and a police car arrived on the scene. A chubby
officer got out, his eyes wide and his mouth in a surprised O.

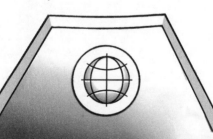

Thor slammed his fists on the hood of the cop car and it folded in half like a taco. The cop drew his weapon, but Funk was already sending a cloud of noxious green air at him. Overcome by the stench, the policeman dropped to his knees.

Miss Information smiled. "Welcome to 1987, where there is no Wi-Fi, iPods, Facebook, or texting. Most people still buy music at a record store."

"What's a record store?" Tammy said.

Miss Information shook her head and pressed a button on the time machine. She watched it collapse and morph into a box she could fit into the palm of her hand. "What a nice feature!"

Benjy floated above her head. "Many of my functions are inoperable, including telecommunications. The satellites needed don't seem to exist."

"But you still have our list of targets, correct?" she asked.

"I do," Benjy said. "In fact, the first one was on that bus."

Miss Information turned her attention to the shaken passengers, who now stood in groups on the side of the road. She spotted a tall, lean elderly man with brown skin and a bristly white mustache. He was rubbing his neck as if he had whiplash.

"Mr. Escala!" she cried, rushing across the street. "Mr. Escala!"

Surprised, the man took a step back. His face was full of fear. "How do you know me?"

"Oh, I don't know you, Mr. Escala, but I've been having a big problem with one of your relatives. Thinking about moving to the United States?"

"My son talks about it," Mr. Escala said. "Who are you? Are you responsible for this accident?"

"Allow us to roll out the welcome wagon," Miss Information said.

Thor picked up a taxicab and threw it down the street. It bounced around like a bowling ball, slamming into a fire hydrant. A geyser of water shot into the air, drenching the crowd.

Mr. Escala's eyes were full of terror.

"The United States is no place for your family," Miss Information said. "This is a lawless country filled with maniacs. You should go to the airport now and get on the first plane home."

Petrified, Mr. Escala ran away.

Ms. Holiday watched him go. "Do you think that will work, Benjy?" she said.

The little orb spun around and clicked. "There is a ninety percent statistical chance that it succeeded. However, the only way to test for accuracy is to go back to our present and see for ourselves."

"No time, Benjy. Who's next?"

"There's a Mr. Dewey working as a mechanic in the year 1995," Benjy said. "Records indicate he's the future father of Duncan Dewey. According to his Facebook page, it appears September first is the day he met Duncan's mother, Aiah."

"Very good," Miss Information said. "Let's go say hello to the happy couple and make sure they become very unhappy."

She set the little box on the ground and it regained its form as the time machine. Moments later, she and the children were spinning their way toward 1995.

21

Ruby slept on a Skee-Ball ramp and woke with a laundry list of aching muscles. Unfortunately, her stiff neck and back were nothing compared to the pain in her face, which had swollen to the size of a party balloon. She was clearly having an allergic reaction, one of her most severe, but for the life of her she could not figure out what kind.

She took two allergy tablets, then searched the pizza parlor for her teammates. She found them with the principal in one of the booths, peering at a large pepperoni pizza. It appeared to be ice-cold.

"There's nothing to eat but pizza, in case you were wondering," Matilda said.

"Cold, ugly, disgusting pizza," Duncan said.

"I'm glad you're awake. We have news," the principal said. "Heathcliff, you're on."

Heathcliff beamed. "Last night, at around eleven P.M., a NASA satellite detected a massive energy spike on our local power grid. Oddly enough, it happened at a school, the Margreet Zelle Detention Center for the Incorrigible. But there's something that makes this even more interesting. The National Weather Service satellite helped me track down the exhaust fumes of Miss Information's flying bus. Guess where the trail ends?"

"The Margreet Zelle Detention Center for the Incorrigible," Ruby guessed.

"And there's more!" Heathcliff said, sinking a token into a nearby arcade game. A moment later, images of Loudmouth, Thor, Funk, and Snot Rocket appeared on-screen. "Guess where these four freaks go to school."

"You found her!" Jackson cried.

"We found her," Heathcliff said. "Miss Information's secret hideout is less than six miles away."

"Suit up, kids. You too, Heathcliff. You're going with them," the principal said.

The boy's grin was as wide as Texas.

Ruby couldn't believe what she was hearing. "I don't think that's a good idea."

"Desperate times call for desperate measures," the principal growled. "Suit up, kids."

Margreet Zelle Detention Center for the Incorrigible looked like Alcatraz prison's baby brother. It had an electrified fence lined with barbed wire, four guard towers, and bars on all the windows.

"Well, it's not Sugarland Academy," Ruby said as she eyed a door with a sign that read SOLITARY CONFINEMENT.

Duncan had his nose buried so deep in the screen of his handheld tracking device that he nearly walked into the wall. "I'm using sonar. There's definitely something deep beneath us. A cave."

"How do we get to it?" Heathcliff asked.

Flinch reached into his pocket and took out a couple of candy bars, which he ate without unwrapping. "I'll just smash through the floor. Give me a second."

"Or we could use this." Duncan opened a locker door.

"No way!" Matilda said.

"Yes way," Duncan said. "Just like ours."

Matilda and Jackson fought to be the first to take the entrance. Ruby followed them, and in a flash she was whisked down a mile-long tunnel and abruptly deposited into the remains of a secret bunker that looked oddly familiar.

"She copied the Playground," Heathcliff said when he landed next to her.

"It's identical," Ruby said.

The walls, columns—even the ceramic tiles—were the same. There was a command center and a desk where Benjamin would hover.

"Ms. Holiday has really taken a leap off the high dive," Jackson said. "She's got her own team of superpowered kids, her own Playground—it's like she's trying to re-create what she once had."

"Could this be a result of the villain virus?" Matilda asked. "Could some of the evil nanobytes have survived and adapted inside her?"

Ruby wasn't sure what to tell Matilda. The information Agent Brand had shared with her and the principal felt private. At the same time, the others deserved to know that their Ms. Holiday was an invention. She decided to tell.

The news seemed to break their hearts as much as it had broken hers.

"Maybe the virus made her crazy," Flinch said.

"Huh?" Ruby replied.

"When you guys were infected with the evil nanobytes, all of you took on new personalities. You also got really smart and invented things you couldn't possibly have created before.

Ms. Holiday already had two personalities: her real identity as a Russian spy, then as our librarian. Actually, if you think about it, she had to pretend to be an American spy, too—"

"This is getting confusing," Matilda said.

"No, I think I understand," Duncan said. "Ms. Holiday was juggling three unique personalities. When she was infected, she took on the fourth—Miss Information. Maybe she couldn't handle another one and something broke."

"So she really *is* sick?" Jackson asked.

"Maybe," Duncan said. "But it would explain why she didn't go back to normal when Flinch destroyed the virus."

A flicker of hope sparked in Ruby's chest. If their former friend was in the midst of a nervous breakdown, perhaps she could be treated.

"What's this?" Jackson said. On the blackened floor there was a large pristine circle.

Duncan removed a device from his backpack. He flipped it on and a needle on its screen bounced around erratically. "The radiation here is off the charts."

"Probably one of her doomsday devices. Think we got lucky and it blew up in her face?" Matilda asked.

Duncan shook his head. "Only if it vaporized her. This circle is completely free of dust or ash. No, it's like something was here . . . and then it wasn't."

"Maybe it's a teleportation device," Heathcliff suggested.

Duncan shrugged. "Maybe. I'll have to turn these readings over to the big brains. They might be able to make something of it."

"Tell them to make us some pizza, too," Flinch said.

"I say we split up and search this place," Heathcliff said. "Miss Information and her goons might have left something behind we can use."

Ruby bristled at Heathcliff's overstep, but it *was* a good idea.

"Fine," she grumbled. "Just stay on the com-links."

The children went their separate ways through the expansive facility. Every room seemed so familiar. It was both creepy and sad for Ruby, since she knew they'd never be able to return to their own headquarters.

She came to what appeared to be an upgrade room. She knew that Miss Information's BULLIES had upgrades, and it made her sick to her stomach that the very thing that made her special could be twisted into something so ugly and dangerous.

"Find anything?"

Ruby jumped. Heathcliff was right behind her.

"Geez . . ."

"Didn't mean to scare you, boss," he said.

Ruby searched her allergies for signs of duplicity. Even though she didn't find any, she was still suspicious. Nanobytes had turned Heathcliff into a terrible monster. Brainstorm, as he once called himself, could literally change reality with a single thought. She didn't like seeing him so close to an upgrade chair.

Ruby sneezed and heard Duncan's voice in her head.

"Hey, guys, I found something!"

"C'mon," she said to Heathcliff, and breathed a sigh of relief when the boy followed her.

They found Duncan hovering over one of the science stations.

"What's that?" Jackson asked, pointing at a huge drawing tacked to a corkboard. It looked like a Frisbee with a wheel in the center. There was also one of the most complicated math equations Ruby had ever seen written alongside it.

"Think that's what caused the explosion?" Flinch asked.

"I have no idea," Duncan said, gesturing to Heathcliff. "But I know someone who might understand it."

Heathcliff studied the drawing.

"What is it?" Jackson said. "Some kind of death ray? An atom smasher? A dinosaur-cloning device?"

Heathcliff scratched his head, then said, "These are the schematics for a time machine."

"A time machine!" Jackson cried. "Evil or not, that's cool!"

"Flinch, pull that down and we'll take it back to the base," Ruby said.

"*Who?*"

Ruby turned to Jackson. "Flinch."

"Who's Flinch?"

"Jackson, he's standing right—"

Ruby turned to where Flinch had been standing, but he was gone.

She turned her head back and forth, searching the room for her missing teammate. All the while the pressure in her head grew. The ache was intense. What was causing the swelling?

"Where did he go? You can't just get up and leave during a mission. Flinch! *Flinch!*"

"Ruby, are you feeling OK?" Matilda asked.

"Where's Flinch?" she said.

Everyone looked at her as if she were smacking herself in the face with a flyswatter while singing "I'm a Little Teapot."

"Ruby, there's no one on the team named Flinch," Duncan said.

Ruby wondered if she was in the middle of a prank but quickly ruled it out. She was allergic to pranks, and besides her fat, agonizing head, she wasn't experiencing any other allergic reactions.

"None of you remember Julio 'Flinch' Escala?" Ruby asked. "Strong kid, eats a lot of candy?"

The other agents looked back at her with mystified expressions.

"Duncan, he's your best friend!" Ruby said.

What was happening? Did her friends really not remember their hyper teammate? No, that wasn't possible, unless . . .

"She's built a time machine!" Ruby shouted, suddenly realizing what her swollen head was trying to tell her.

"I know where Ms. Holiday and the BULLIES have gone," she said. Her teammates looked at her, and she took a deep breath. "August 16, 1987."

END TRANSMISSION.

TOP SECRET DOSSIER

CODE NAME: RAGS THE WONDERMUTT
REAL NAME: RAGS
YEARS ACTIVE: 1983-84
CURRENT OCCUPATION:
UNKNOWN

HISTORY: RAGS WAS NOT THE
ONLY ANIMAL TO BE ON
THE NERDS ROSTER, BUT HE WAS
THE FIRST. FOUND OUTSIDE NATHAN
HALE ELEMENTARY, THIS STRAY
POOCH STOLE THE HEART OF THE
ENTIRE TEAM AND SOON SPENT HIS
NIGHTS EATING PUPPY CHOW AND
SLEEPING IN THE PLAYGROUND.
ONE NIGHT, WHILE THE TEAM WAS
ON A MISSION, RAGS WANDERED
INTO THE UPGRADE ROOM. HE
EMERGED JUST AS STINKY BUT
WAS FASTER AND STRONGER AND
HAD A MONSTROUS BITE.

UPGRADE: WITH THE UPGRADES,
RAGS NOT ONLY CHASED CARS BUT
NOW COULD CATCH THEM. WITH
HIS SUPER-ENHANCED TEETH AND
JAWS, HE ONCE STOPPED A TANK
THAT WAS BARRELING TOWARD
THOMAS KNOWLTON MIDDLE SCHOOL.
UNFORTUNATELY, RAGS SANK HIS
TEETH INTO THE WING OF A SPACE
SHUTTLE AS IT WAS TAKING OFF
AND WAS NEVER SEEN AGAIN.

LEVEL 8
ACCESS GRANTED

BEGIN TRANSMISSION:

22

38°50' N, 77°3' W

Heathcliff watched Ruby's face fill with desperation. She looked frantic and overexcited. Yes, she was uptight, controlling, and bossy, but she was usually the calmest person on the team. Seeing her so freaked out made him nervous.

"Flinch doesn't exist anymore!" she cried.

"Maybe you should sit down," the principal said.

"NO!" she shouted. "I checked all the computers. Julio Escala was never a member of this team. In fact, he was never even born."

Ruby paced back and forth. "I know what you're thinking, but you're wrong. I'm not crazy. We're in the middle of a crisis, people. And we need to move fast."

"Where?" Matilda asked.

"I told you! 1987!"

"Why do you think that?" Duncan said.

Ruby pointed to her swollen noggin. "The allergies don't lie! I think I'm allergic to something big—something like my friends vanishing from existence. I don't know. This one's not part of the 8,765 cataloged reactions my upgrades can detect."

"Ruby, you need to calm down. Back up and try to help us understand," Heathcliff said.

Ruby snatched him by the collar. "She erased him!"

"First, you're choking me to death. Second, I don't know what you're talking about," Heathcliff said, trying to pull himself away and failing. For a wiry girl, Ruby Peet was strong.

"Ruby, you're tired. We were up late last night searching—"

"Yes! That's it! I can prove it. Remember that news clipping we found? The one from 1987 that had a photo with Miss Information and the BULLIES in it? Follow me!"

Heathcliff followed her through the maze of arcade games. Suddenly, Ruby started pumping tokens into the one they had been using the previous night. She tapped a few buttons and pulled on the joystick and the old newspaper article they had found reappeared. There was the photo of the car accident with Ms. Holiday, Tessa, and the BULLIES.

"The computer glitch," Heathcliff said.

"No!" Ruby shouted. "I know I told you that you were causing the software to overload, but what if you weren't? What if this is an actual picture of Ms. Holiday and Tessa Lipton?"

"That's not possible," Duncan said.

"Someone from Flinch's family must have been at this accident!" she cried, pointing at the photo. "She's changed the past. She's erased our friend."

"Listen, I love *Doctor Who* as much as the next guy, but time travel isn't possible," the principal said.

"You still don't believe me? Then how do you explain this?" she asked, waving the drafting paper they had found in the evil Playground.

"What is it?" the principal said.

Heathcliff took it and smoothed out the wrinkles. His eyes

grew big. His heart began to race. He felt like he might pass out. "She built a time machine!" he cried. The more he read, the more he realized that the woman hadn't *tried* to build a time machine . . . she *had* built a time machine.

"And she's using it to erase us one by one," Ruby cried out in a panic.

Heathcliff tried to calm his breathing. "I—I think Ruby's right. I think she might be allergic to changes in the space-time continuum. That might be why she remembers this Flinch kid and we don't."

"That's what I've been trying to tell you! My allergies have been going haywire all day."

"So what do we do?" Duncan said. Ruby pointed to the designs. "We need our own time machine. We need to go back and stop her. Heathcliff, you get the scientists started on these plans while the rest of us go get him."

"Who is 'him'?" Matilda asked.

"The world's worst oboe player!"

23

Alexander Brand was trying to write a song about his feelings. He had decided early on that it should be a country-and-western song because all the best songs about broken hearts were country-and-western. The lyrics would have to be about a bad librarian who liked to break a man's heart before dashing off to do it to someone else. He even decided on a name for the song: "The Screwy Decimal System." Unfortunately, the song had three strikes against it. First, you can't play a sad country-and-western song on an oboe. Second, Brand was the furthest thing from a poet. And third, his singing was almost as bad as his oboe playing.

He carried the instrument out to the dock and sat down on the folding chair. He inserted the reed into his mouth, inhaled, and began to play a few jerky notes. Then he stopped and sang.

She fined my heart like an overdue book.
Threw me on the shelving cart without a second look.
I've walked a sad road all across this nation,
And I can't get my heart back into circulation.

"You really are bad at the oboe, boss."

He didn't have to see who it was. He recognized Ruby's stubborn voice.

He turned to face her.

Duncan, Matilda, Jackson, and the principal stood next to her. Duncan had a handkerchief in his hands and the principal was holding a length of rope. Ruby held the costume head of a cartoon mouse in her hands.

"Your girlfriend built a time machine," Ruby said. "She's gone back to muck up the past. She's already erased a member of the team. This is the biggest threat we have ever faced, and we need your help."

Brand shook his head. "I already told you I wouldn't go back," he grumbled.

"OK, well, don't say I didn't try to be nice," Ruby said. She reached into her pocket and pulled out a small aerosol can, aimed it at his face, and sprayed. A white mist filled his nose and mouth.

"What is this?" But he knew what it was. He'd seen it in the Playground. It was going to make him sleepy. Very, very sleepy.

Duncan shoved the handkerchief into his mouth, and the principal tied his hands. A moment later the costumed head of a cartoon rat plunged him into darkness.

24

38°53' N, 77°1' W

People in the diner were staring.

"What? You've never seen a woman in a skull mask eating a slice of pie before?" Miss Information asked.

They turned their eyes back to their meals, though they shot nervous glances at her from time to time.

"I don't think it's you," Snot Rocket whispered. "I think it's your boyfriend."

Miss Information cuddled up to the scarecrow. "Ah, 1995," she said. "So quaint. Don't you just love the clothes and the hair, Alex? Everyone is so unkempt."

"When are we going to get to work?" Funk asked. The boy had refused to order anything and sat with his arms crossed.

"Sweetie pie, you *are* working," she said. "We've already checked off one of our targets."

ATTACK OF THE BULLIES

"I have no idea what you're talking about," Funk said, steamed. "We harassed some Mexican guy and hopped around on that time machine, and all we have to show for it is a bunch of upset stomachs."

Thor still looked a little pale.

Miss Information pointed her fork at Funk's face. "That Mexican guy was the grandfather of one of our enemies. His son and daughter-in-law had two children, and one of them happened to be the hyperactive strong boy who kicked your butts at the White House. Well, guess what? He was never born—at least not in the United States. He's not in D.C., he doesn't have superstrength, and he didn't beat you up yesterday. We literally bullied him out of existence. You're giving the future an atomic wedgie it'll never forget!"

The BULLIES cheered—all except for Tessa.

Miss Information watched her closely. When Tessa noticed, she smiled weakly.

"So, what are we doing in 1995?" Tammy asked.

"We're here to interrupt a first date," she said.

Benjy floated out of the paper bag that was lying on the table.

Diners rose from their seats and made a beeline for the exit.

"Aiah Dewey met her husband, the father of one Duncan

Dewey, on this day in this diner . . . And here she comes now," Miss Information said as bells jingled on the front door.

In walked Aiah, a beautiful seventeen-year-old. She and her gaggle of friends giggled and chatted until they saw Miss Information's mask, the floating ball, and the scarecrow. Their laughter stopped, and they tentatively took a booth in the back of the restaurant, as far from the motley crew as possible.

"Tessa, you're up," she said. "Our Romeo should be along any minute."

Tessa nodded and went to work on her face. A few twists here, a few turns there, and soon she was the mirror image of Aiah Dewey. Even her hair was identical.

There was another jingle at the door and a tall, handsome teenager walked into the diner. He wore a white T-shirt and jeans covered in grease smears.

"Hey, Avery," a waitress said. "How's the car?"

"You've got a busted water pump, Rose," he replied.

The waitress frowned. "How much is that going to cost?"

Avery smiled. "Next to nothing. I pulled one out of a junker at the dump. It's like new. You'll be able to drive it home tonight."

Rose's face lit up. "Avery, you're the best. How much do I owe you?"

"One chocolate milk shake and we'll call it even," he said.

"All right, Tessa," Miss Information muttered. "You need to do something before he sees the real Aiah."

"He seems like a nice guy," Tessa said. "We're wrecking his life."

"A guy like that will find someone else," Miss Information said. "You're not having second thoughts, are you? If you want your dad to go to prison, we can just go back. It's really up to you."

Tessa nodded and got out of the booth.

Miss Information watched her walk over to Avery. She flashed him a smile and he flashed one back.

"Here you go, Avery," the waitress said, handing him a large glass filled to the top with chocolaty goodness, whipped cream, and a cherry on top.

"Thanks, Rose," he said.

"No, thank *you*," Rose said before moving away to pour coffee for a customer at the counter.

"So . . . I hear you fix things," Tessa said.

Avery nodded.

Tessa took the milk shake from his hand and poured it on his head. It dribbled down his face and all over his clothes.

"Well, fix this," Tessa said.

Avery sputtered and grabbed a handful of napkins from a dispenser. He wiped the drink out of his eyes. "Are you crazy?"

"Yes, I'm crazy. You should stay away from me, Avery," Tessa said, then she turned toward the team. "Let's get out of here."

Funk's face grew big and toothy. "That was epic."

Miss Information grinned and got to her feet. "All right, team! That's two down, three to go. Who's next, Benjy?"

The little ball clicked and buzzed. "According to bank statements, Ben Choi, father of Matilda 'Wheezer' Choi, purchased a ticket to South Korea for a flight leaving at 2:35 P.M. on September 14, 1990. It is on this trip that he met his future wife, Matilda's mother."

"Unless, of course, some kind of trouble occurs at the airport," Miss Information said.

END TRANSMISSION.

TOP SECRET DOSSIER

CODE NAME: THIRD DEGREE
REAL NAME: AMOS "JUNIOR" CASTO
YEARS ACTIVE: 2001–07
CURRENT OCCUPATION:
CEO OF HAWAIIAN TROPIC
SUNTAN LOTION CORP

HISTORY: AMOS'S PALE SKIN WAS HIGHLY SUSCEPTIBLE TO SUNBURN. FIVE MINUTES OUTSIDE WITHOUT APPLYING AN INCH-THICK LAYER OF SUNSCREEN AND HE WOULD TURN INTO A FLAMING-HOT TOMATO. SOME STUDIES SHOWED THAT STANDING NEXT TO THE BOY WAS ENOUGH FOR A PERSON TO CONTRACT A VICIOUS RED BURN. MOST OF THE SKIN DAMAGE OCCURRED ON THE LOWER HALVES OF HIS ARMS AND LEGS AND ON HIS NECK, DUE TO THE SHORT-SLEEVED SHIRTS AND CUTOFF JEANS HE WORE EVERY DAY.

UPGRADE: THIRD DEGREE'S BURNS
WERE ENHANCED SO THAT THEY
GENERATED HEAT, ALLOWING HIM
TO START RAGING BONFIRES
WHENEVER NEEDED.

LEVEL 9
ACCESS GRANTED

BEGIN TRANSMISSION:

25

38°50' N, 77°3' W

The NERDS and the principal dragged Agent Brand into Marty Mozzarella's, which was mercifully deserted for the night. Brand still wore the big mouse head and was groaning indignantly.

The principal waved the children a safe distance away. "He's angry. I'm going to take the head off and then the gag, so be careful of his teeth."

Brand blinked hard against the restaurant's harsh fluorescent lighting. As soon as the gag came out, so did a tirade of potty language not appropriate for print. Ruby waited patiently for him to stop, but there seemed to be no end in sight. When he didn't calm down, she took the gag from the principal and stuffed it back into Brand's mouth.

"Sorry, boss, but we have to act fast. Here's what's happening. Ms. Holiday has built a playground just like ours."

"Identical," Matilda said.

"She's assembled a team of kids just like us," Ruby said.

"They even have upgrades," Jackson said.

"They call themselves the BULLIES," Duncan said.

"Her science team created a time machine," Ruby said. "She's already erased one of our members, a kid named Flinch, who you won't remember because he never existed, and now she's probably going after the four of us."

"You mean three," the principal said.

"Huh?"

"There's only three of you on the team, unless you're counting Heathcliff, but he's just helping."

Ruby looked around at her friends. "Where's Duncan?"

"Who?" Matilda asked.

"Duncan Dewey! Agent Gluestick!"

The others gave her the increasingly familiar *You're going crazy* look.

"Aaargh!" Ruby shouted, then turned her attention back to Brand. "Your girlfriend just erased Duncan Dewey! I know you don't remember him, but he was a really nice guy."

Brand moaned something unintelligible through his gag.

"Shush!" Ruby snapped. "I know you want to sit up at your

stupid cabin and scare away the wildlife with your oboe, but you might be able to reach whatever is left of Ms. Holiday, so you're helping whether you want to or not."

Ruby looked to the principal.

He nodded. "Yeah, what she said."

Ruby removed the handkerchief from Brand's mouth. The former spy took a long, frustrated breath. "Well, I guess that's settled."

Ruby smiled.

"Heathcliff, you're on!" the principal shouted.

Heathcliff raced into the room, arms filled with papers and a calculator. He came to a screeching halt in front of Mr. Brand. He peered into the former spy's shaggy face.

"What happened to him?"

Brand growled and Heathcliff jumped back.

"Where are we with our time machine?" the principal asked as he untied Brand's hands.

"Well, first of all, whoever designed Ms. Holiday's time machine was a real knucklehead. I mean, it's genius, but every time she turns it on, it threatens to destroy the universe. It's obvious that it's based on the Decoyer Loop Universe theory, which is like so last year, but—"

"Can you turn the science down to one and the English up to ten?" Jackson asked.

"Yeah, sorry," Heathcliff said. "Basically, her time machine rips a huge hole in space-time, which could have some nasty side effects. Black holes. Supernovas. Plus, it's a dirty technology and bad for the environment. I threw out her entire design and started over with a pet theory of mine. I have always believed there are tiny tears in the space-time continuum—little dimples, if you can imagine. Turns out I'm right. They're all over the place, and we can stretch one so it's big enough to travel through. It's much safer, and we don't need a huge machine."

"So how do we find one of these holes?" Matilda asked.

"Already done," Heathcliff said. "There's one right here in this restaurant."

He gestured to the multicolored ball pit at the center of the room. A tangle of tubes connected a huge pulsating engine to the pit. "I've attached it to a low-grade nuclear power source. I'm charging the battery cells now. It should be ready soon."

"OK, I know I'm the C-minus member of this team, but even with a time machine, how are we going to find her?" Jackson asked. "Miss Information and her toad squad could have gone anywhere. Or 'anywhen.'"

"She allowed herself to be photographed during her trip to August 16, 1987. Something she and her team did there erased . . . what was his name again?"

"Flinch," Ruby said.

"Yes, Flinch. All we have to do is go back to that day and stop her plan and we get Flinch and Gluestick back in one shot," Heathcliff explained.

"I can't do this," Brand said.

Ruby turned to him, fully prepared to unleash every ounce of her anger and frustration. His broken heart was not going to get in the way of her being born. She'd put him back in the mouse suit if he wouldn't cooperate.

". . . unless you let me shave," Brand continued. "If I'm going to stop my ex from ruining the world, I want to look hot."

While the remnants of her team waited for the time machine to boot up, Ruby sat at an arcade game and searched police records for news of her disappearance from home. What she found was worse than she'd imagined. Her mother and father had appeared on the nightly news, Grandpa Saul had done an interview with the *Washington Post*, and her cousins had built a Find Ruby Peet website. Her disappearance had gone viral, and hundreds of people were searching all over Arlington for her. She couldn't stand knowing the suffering she was putting her family through. She felt like crying, remembering the last conversation she had with her mom and dad.

But then she found a newspaper article with a photograph

of her house. Parked on the street was a familiar black car and behind the steering wheel was the same Secret Service agent who had taken her to see the president. The principal was right. They were watching her house, probably tapping the phones, and waiting to pounce if they got so much as a hint that Ruby was reaching out.

At that moment, she would've been happy to open up any drawer her nieces and nephews wanted to explore. She would let them tear apart her socks and ignore her TV remote instructions and build forts in her bedroom with filthy bricks. She wanted nothing more than to watch her big, loud, obnoxious family turn the house into a complete and total mess. Especially now, when there was a good chance she could be wiped out of existence at any moment. Then they wouldn't be searching far and wide for her—they'd forget her completely. Somehow that was even worse.

"We're ready," Heathcliff said, approaching her cautiously.

"Brand?"

"He just finished. I wonder if I had forty minutes with a barber, manicurist, and a tailor if I would look that handsome."

"It's really hard for you. Isn't it?" she asked him.

"What?"

"Not having a family," she said.

Heathcliff's shoulders slumped, and he nodded. "Sometimes

I feel like I'm a boat on the ocean and I can't find land no matter which direction I sail."

Ruby looked back at an image of her family's worried faces on the news. She didn't know what kind of life she might have in the future, but if she could fix all her problems, she'd never complain about a crowded house again.

The team gathered at the ball pit. Ruby's glands ached, and she looked around warily. "Where's Matilda?" Ruby asked.

Jackson, Heathcliff, the principal, and Brand just stared at her.

"Not another one!" Ruby exclaimed. "We have to do this fast. Let's move!"

Heathcliff adjusted some dials and checked a pressure valve. "One of us has to stay here and keep an eye on this machine. It needs a lot of power, some of which I'm pulling off the local grid. If the lights go out, our connection will be cut and we could be lost in time permanently."

"And who is that going to be?" the principal said.

Everyone looked at Heathcliff.

"Me? No way!"

"Heathcliff!" Ruby cried.

"My life is at risk, too, right? If anyone should stay, it's one of the grown-ups. She's after team members, not staff!"

"Hodges, I need the most capable people on this mission,"

the principal said. "Ruby and Jackson have upgrades. Brand is a trained secret agent. I was a Golden Gloves winner growing up in New Jersey."

"And my argument is that you should stay and watch the machine," Heathcliff said.

"Me?"

"Yes, you. Of all the people associated with this team, Miss Information has the least grudge against you. If she even bothers to prevent your birth, she's going to do it last."

The principal growled. "Aargh! He's right. Brand, I hate this job. I need to crush some skulls! I can't remember the last time I gave someone a concussion! Once this is over, I'm resigning. I'll go back to the kitchen. I miss my spatula!"

Brand looked at Heathcliff. "Looks like you're along for the ride, kid. How does this machine work?"

Heathcliff beamed. "All you have to do is jump in."

Brand eyed the multicolored balls. "Of course," he groaned.

Using his cane, he crawled into the center of the balls.

"Get down in there," Heathcliff said.

"Is there no end to my humiliation?" Brand fell onto his back and let the balls swallow him.

"Looks like it works," Jackson said.

"I was a little worried he'd be sucked into a miniature black hole. If so, his entire body would have been crushed by an intense gravity. And we'd have had to watch the whole thing," Heathcliff confessed.

"Get going while you still can, Heathcliff," Ruby ordered.

Heathcliff snatched his backpack and leaped into the pit. A moment later he was gone, too.

Ruby's head suddenly felt as if someone had hooked a bicycle pump to it and was filling it full of air. "All right, Jackson. You're up."

"Who?" the principal asked.

Ruby whipped around, looking for her teammate and his amazing braces, but he was gone. If she didn't want to be next, she had to act fast. She dove under the balls and suddenly felt as if she were sinking into a huge Jell-O mold. There was a shimmering feeling to the air and a coppery taste in her mouth like she was sucking on a penny, and then—BAM!—she was gone.

The trip felt a little like the times she had dropped into the Playground from her school locker. But this tube seemed to be made of light and stars that branched off like the veins in a human body. The tunnels led to endless possibilities; one might take her to the dawn of man, another to Earth's final days. There were millions of destinations. She hoped she'd stay on course. Things would go from bad to worse if she landed in the time of dinosaurs.

Suddenly, she hit something. It was hard and cold and

smelled a lot like pizza. She pulled her head out of the balls. Brand and Heathcliff were waiting by the side of the pit, but the restaurant looked exactly as it did a moment ago.

"It didn't work," she said. "It was supposed to take us to the street that Miss Information and the BULLIES arrived on in 1987."

"No, it worked," Brand said. He pointed to a table full of kids happily munching on pizza. They wore faded bell-bottom jeans and platform shoes. They looked like extras from a TV show her dad loved called *The Brady Bunch*. At one table, the kids wore tie-dyed T-shirts and pants covered in rhinestones. She'd seen clothes like these in her grandmother's closet. Oddly enough, the restaurant looked exactly the same as it did in her time, except the video games had been replaced by pinball machines.

"This is what people wore in 1987?" she asked.

"We're not in 1987. We're in 1977," Heathcliff said.

"*1977?* Why did you send us so far back?"

"That was my idea," Brand said. "A girl with super-allergies, a boy genius, and a spy with a bum leg are no match for five superpowered kids and a crazy woman. We need help from kids who know how to handle these kinds of situations. Unfortunately, the NERDS team of 1987 was trapped in an ice prison by Dr. Frostbite that summer. So we're going to recruit some new teammates—namely, the greatest NERDS team ever assembled. The first one."

"You mean Four Eyes, Macramé, Ghost, Beanpole, and Static Cling?" Ruby cried as her heart did a backflip. She had studied the case files; she knew everything about every agent who had ever been in NERDS. If there was a team that could help them with the BULLIES, it was the NERDS of 1977.

26

38°52' N, 77°6' W

Rupert P. Breckinridge III looked
at his teammates and grimaced. They were a collection of sharp
elbows, bony knees, runny noses, scabs, and insecurity. If their
job was to protect the world, then the world was in serious
trouble.

"Is there no better way to get into this facility? This is
insanity!" Special Director Preston shouted after a tube had
deposited him into a leather chair.

Rupert had been in that tube himself, and he knew it wasn't
a fun ride, nor was cramming into the locker to get to it.

Preston retrieved a shoe that had come off during the trip,
then took off his horn-rimmed glasses and rubbed them on his
pant leg. One of his pens was leaking in the pocket of his white
short-sleeved work shirt. A piece of toilet paper was stuck to the

back of the poor man's pant leg. Rupert sighed. The boss was a bigger nerd than his agents.

"In three weeks, the school above this facility will open and you will begin attending classes with the rest of the children. When that day comes, the five of you will be officially activated and sent on missions, so we need to double-time your training. Let's get back to our karate practice." He took out a book titled *Karate for Beginners* and flipped through its pages.

Rupert wondered, not for the first time, why Preston had been put in charge of a group of superpowered agents. Sure, he was a spy—but most of his work had been in code breaking. He had no practical mission experience, no hand-to-hand combat training, and his karate knowledge came from watching *Hong Kong Phooey* cartoons.

"Aww, man!" came a predictable whine from Carmello Gotti, an Italian kid so pudgy he might have been made out of dough. Rupert had heard that before being recruited onto the team, Carmello hadn't so much as thrown a ball. Now he had special implants in his gigantic round hairdo that fired massive blasts of static electricity. "Can't we do something else? My parents are getting suspicious of all the bruises."

"No, they're not. They assume what everyone else assumes— that Billy Dunkleman is beating you up again," came the sharp, sarcastic voice of May Price. Her wit was almost as fast as her fingers, which were supercharged with special gloves, allowing her to knit anything she could imagine out of yarn. Preston called her Agent Macramé.

"Burn!" Mikey Buckley said as he burst into laughter. He was as skinny as a cornstalk and had a brain for technology. He still hadn't chosen a code name he considered cool enough but was toying around with "Fantastic Boy."

"You guys are mean," Minnie Dupont said. The tiny girl pressed a button on her jacket and vanished. Agent Ghost had a very cool power, and as far as Rupert could tell, she was the only one with a skill that could be valuable for spying. Unfortunately, she was brutally shy.

"People! We need to focus," Director Preston said meekly, but he was ignored while the agents argued for another ten minutes.

Rupert sighed. The NERDS were never going to become a team. They didn't even like one another, and all of them had scored zero on the self-confidence meter. It was a shame, really. When Rupert was recruited, he was sure the group would change his life. But it looked like he was headed back to the mundane world he came from, the one where he was chased home everyday by Matt Phaltz, the psychopath who enjoyed ripping the waistbands out of Rupert's Fruit of the Looms. Well, Rupert liked his waistbands. He refused to go back!

What they needed was a James Bond type, a leader, someone the others could respect. If Preston couldn't motivate the team, Rupert would do it himself. He flipped down one of the many lenses on his special glasses and a blast of white energy shot out of his eyes, causing a nearby wall to crumble.

"QUIET!" he shouted. "You kids are the most intolerable, unprofessional, frustrating, lazy, and cranky dweebs I have ever met. Mr. Preston has tried everything—pep talks, being your friend, being your enemy, being a drill instructor, begging, bribery—and none of it has worked. You bicker endlessly. You skip training sessions. You aren't even sure how to use your gadgets. You treat this headquarters like it's some kind of . . . some kind of playground!"

Preston blinked. "Yeah!" he cried.

Rupert pushed his glasses up on the bridge of his nose and looked around. "You might be perfectly happy to go out on a mission and get yourselves killed, but I have no plans to join you. So here's the deal: Take this seriously or quit and go back to being the pathetic, bullied misfits you were six weeks ago."

The threat seemed to have the desired affect. The thought of having to return to their normal lives, without the gadgets, was more than the NERDS could imagine. Each one tried to stand a little taller.

"Goodness gracious!" Preston shouted when he discovered

his ruined shirt. "Let's take five while I find something else to wear."

He dashed off, leaving the children alone.

"OK, he's useless," Rupert said. "So if we're going to learn to fight, it's up to us. Each one of us has a skill, and if we work together, we can be unstoppable. That's why they chose us. So let's get back to training! Who's with me?"

Rupert could have heard a pin drop.

Minnie raised her hand. "Um, I gotta get going."

"Yeah, me too," added May. "*The Gong Show* is on in fifteen minutes."

"I've got work to do on Benjamin," Mikey said.

"Are you still working on that stupid calculator?" May asked.

The boy grew defensive. "It's called a computer, and someday it will be a huge asset. I'm programming it with all the knowledge of one of America's greatest spies—Benjamin Franklin. It's going to talk, and think, and help with mission reports. I've already figured out how to make it fly!"

He pressed a button and a massive machine at the far end of the room let out a chorus of screaming gears as it rose off the floor: one inch, then two, then three—then it came crashing to the floor.

"Way to go, Fantastic Boy," Carmello quipped.

The team shuffled toward the exit tubes.

Rupert took one of the tubes up to his locker. The hallway was empty except for a crew of janitors screwing in lightbulbs and touching up paint jobs in preparation for the first day of school. He was glad *something* was almost ready.

"Hey, Four Eyes!" a voice shouted the moment Rupert stepped outside the school.

Rupert cringed. It was *Matt Phaltz*!

He took off running without looking back but could hear Phaltz and his friends running close behind. They were shouting and laughing as they chased him down the street.

"Leave me alone," he cried, but they ignored his plea. He made a sharp turn at the corner and was nearly home when he tripped over a garden hose someone had left lying on the sidewalk. He fell hard, bruising his knees and wrists, and before he knew it, the bullies were on top of him, trying to de-pants him right there in the middle of the street.

"C'mon, guys! Leave me alone," he begged. The thought occurred to him to flip his laser lense down on his glasses and blast the bullies to kingdom come, but he and the others had vowed not to use their gadgets on civilians. It would blow their cover, and their devices were too dangerous. But that didn't mean he had to take a beating.

He pulled his fist back and swung. Matt Phaltz went sprawling across the sidewalk with a puffy eye. The only problem was, Rupert had missed. His fist had never connected with the bully.

Dumbfounded, Rupert looked around just in time to see Phaltz's toadie Mitch crumple to the ground, followed by Ty and Paulie—all at the hands of a nerdy girl with glasses and poofy yellow hair, a redheaded kid who was probably half the size of Phaltz, and a man in a black tuxedo, holding a cane.

The girl smiled. "I hope you don't mind, Four Eyes. I'm allergic to bullies."

"Who are you?" Rupert asked.

"Ruby Peet, and let me say what an honor it is to meet one of the greatest members of NERDS that ever lived. I've read all your files and—"

Rupert flipped the laser lens on his glasses and prepared to fight. His secret was out, and clearly these enemy agents had been sent to kill him and the others. "I don't know who you are, but you won't take me alive," Rupert said. He'd heard someone say that on an episode of *S.W.A.T.* It seemed appropriate.

"We're not here to hurt you, Rupert," the boy said.

Rupert could feel the heat in his glasses as his laser prepared to fire. "I asked you who you are. Someone better start talking!"

The man hobbled forward. "My name is Agent Alexander Brand, and I'm the director of the National Espionage, Rescue, and Defense Society from the twenty-first century."

"The twenty-first century!"

"Some bad guys are coming and only you can help us stop them," Ruby said.

"How can I help you? I don't get activated for three weeks!"

"We need you, pal," their redheaded friend said. "And we need your team—the greatest fighting force the world has ever seen."

27

38°52' N, 77°6' W

"Next thing she's going to tell us is she's from outer space. Do you know Luke Skywalker, too?" Carmello said when Rupert's team had reassembled to hear Ruby, Agent Brand, and Heathcliff plead their case.

"Wow, you are even more annoying than your file suggests," Ruby said to the boy.

"If you're NERDS from the future, show us your gadgets," May said.

Ruby looked at Heathcliff, then back at the kids. "We don't have gadgets. *We're* the gadgets. I'm filled with these things called nanobytes and—"

"Nano-what?" Minnie whispered.

"Microscopic robots that enhance our weaknesses," Heathcliff said.

"Fascinating," Mikey said.

"Oh, yeah?" Carmello said to Heathcliff. "What can *you* do?"

"Well, um . . . I used to have these big buck teeth and I could hypnotize anyone who looked at them, but they got knocked out and now I'm in between powers . . . but Ruby's got superallergies," Heathcliff said defensively.

"Superallergies!" Carmello shouted. "The future sounds pretty bogus. I'm going home to play Pong."

Ruby stepped in front of Carmello. "All right, big guy. You want proof: Try to get past me."

"I would never hit a girl or a person wearing glasses, and you're both."

Carmello tried to step past her, but Ruby stopped him with a punch to his flabby chest.

"Ow! That hurt!"

"Keep coming," she said.

"I'm not fooling," Carmello roared. "If you hit me again, I'll—"

Before he could finish, Ruby slapped him in the face five times.

"I'm allergic to empty threats," she said.

Carmello stomped his feet like an overgrown toddler. His face was red from anger and welts. "Fine!" he shouted, charging like an angry bull. Ruby leaped up and roundhouse-kicked him in the face. He fell down hard and stayed there.

"Let's see her attack a smaller target," Minnie said, activating her cloak.

Heathcliff watched Ruby move with lightning speed and land thunderous punches at what looked like nothing but air. She spun around and there was an "Oof." She shot her knee upward and there was an "Aargh." She jabbed a wicked uppercut and then there was a *thump* followed by a weak "I quit."

When Minnie reappeared, she was on the floor with the beginnings of a black eye. "I believe her," she croaked.

"This is a very important mission. The people we are going to confront are dangerous. Can we count on you?" Brand asked the bewildered kids.

Rupert nodded. "We're in. We've only got one problem," Rupert said. "We're actually really lousy spies."

"The worst," Mikey said.

Ruby looked at Heathcliff and Agent Brand. "What can we teach them before I disappear?"

Heathcliff, Ruby, and Brand led the NERDS into a training room. Heathcliff was thrilled not only to meet such legends but also to feel like a full member of the team once again. Ruby was no longer giving him meaningless jobs to keep him busy.

Brand taught the children all he could about submission holds, pressure points, using leverage against opponents, and using their minds to combat muscles. His years of secret-agent training and knowledge of dozens of fighting styles were spread out before the freshman spies, and Heathcliff hoped they would take advantage of what they learned.

Ruby focused on intelligence, preparing the children for the environment they would soon visit and going over all the information about the BULLIES and Miss Information she had collected.

Heathcliff turned his attention to each of the children's gadgets, helping them understand their capabilities, and even managed to find new ways to use them. Rupert could combine lenses to produce a bright flash that could temporarily blind an opponent. He expanded Macramé's handiwork from yarn and knitting needles to rope and wire and even discovered she could chisel away at hardened concrete with her superfast hands. He taught Ghost how to expand her cloaking technology to hide other people and objects as big as cars. He taught Static Cling how to create a charge in his hair that he could hold and build in strength, making his electrical blast infinitely stronger. Mikey wanted to be known as Fantastic Boy for his ability to invent gadgets on the fly. Unfortunately, of all the agents, he was the most vulnerable in a fight.

"So," Mikey said, grim-faced. They sat before a workstation he was using to create his inventions. "I sort of stink."

Heathcliff shook his head. He knew exactly how Mikey felt. "No, you have the best gadget of the bunch. You've got a very imaginative brain. Your head will probably save the world more than the other gadgets combined. What have you been working on? Maybe there's something here that you can use as a weapon."

Mikey showed him a long stick with a claw on the end. When he pushed a button on its tip, the claw contracted. "It's for getting things off of high shelves. I call it the Gator Grabber."

"Um, probably not going to be much help unless your bad guy is hiding on top of a Christmas tree," Heathcliff said. "What else?"

Mikey handed him what looked like a harpoon gun with a plunger on the end. "This is the Suction Gun. It's also for getting things off of high shelves."

"Right," Heathcliff said as he tried to hide his nervousness. "You seem to have a thing about high shelves."

"I'm tall, so everyone asks me to get things for them," Mikey grumbled. "I build these things so people will leave me alone."

"OK, but we need something that might be intimidating," Heathcliff said.

"Oh! I got it!" Mikey scooped up what looked like a pair of Moon Boots made of metal. He slipped them on his feet and grinned. "What do you think? I call them Extend-o-boots. They're designed to help you get—"

"—things off of high shelves?"

Mikey nodded, then frowned. "Yeah."

Heathcliff forced a smile. "Maybe your skills are better suited for communications or planning."

Mikey nodded. "Maybe you're right." He leaned over to take off the boots, and with a loud "Oops!" the boots extended him thirty feet off the ground on two spindly stilts.

Heathcliff craned his neck to look up at the boy. "Wow!"

"Sorry, the trigger is pretty sensitive," Mikey said as the stilts lowered him back to the floor.

"How high can those go?"

"About forty feet," the boy shouted. "But I could design them to go as high as a hundred. Why?"

"I think we've found something we can use," Heathcliff said. "These amazing boots make you into some kind of butt-kicking beanpole. In fact, that would be a great code name for you—Agent Beanpole!"

The boy scowled as he descended to his normal height. "That's the dumbest code name I've ever heard."

"Well, they can't all be winners. They used to call me Choppers—wait, what's that?" Heathcliff asked, pointing to the massive silver box behind the desk.

"Benjamin!" Mikey cried. He pushed a button on the box's side and it glowed with a blue light. "It's called a computer. The other guys think I'm wasting my time, but someday it will help the team with its missions—if I can ever get it working."

Heathcliff removed his backpack and took out the two halves of Benjamin he was trying to reassemble. "You're *not* wasting your time."

Mikey took the pieces and examined them closely. "This is *my* work. I mean, it's super tiny, but this motherboard is my design! It works! Benjamin *works!*"

"Actually, it doesn't at the moment. It's damaged. I almost had it working again, but I had a setback," Heathcliff said.

Mikey put on a set of goggles with thick lenses. "Well, it needs some wiring replacement, but I see a problem already. You've got a conductor in the wrong position."

He took a set of tweezers and went to work on the robot's inner workings. Heathcliff heard a *click* and then Mikey handed it back.

"That should do the trick. I've got some copper wiring over there if you need any, and feel free to use my tools. I'd love to see how he turned out."

Heathcliff grabbed a few things he would need, thanked Beanpole, and shoved Benjamin into his backpack just as May approached.

"Agent Brand says we need to go. We're about as ready as we're gonna get," she said.

END TRANSMISSION.

TOP SECRET DOSSIER

CODE NAME: UNCLE MITCH
REAL NAME: MITCH CASTO
ACTIVE: 1998
CURRENT OCCUPATION:
MANAGER OF
A WAVERUNNER COMPANY

HISTORY: MITCH, THE UNCLE OF
FORMER AGENT AMOS "JUNIOR"
CASTO, DISCOVERED THE PLAYGROUND
WHILE SPYING ON HIS NEPHEW'S
AFTER-SCHOOL ACTIVITIES. HE GOT
TRAPPED INSIDE THE UPGRADE
ROOM, WHERE IT WAS DETERMINED
HIS BIGGEST WEAKNESSES WERE HIS
HANDLEBAR MUSTACHE AND
THIN COMB-OVER HAIRCUT. HE
WAS GIVEN THE NANOBYTE VERSION
OF A TRIM AND A SHAVE, EMERGING
WITH HAIR PLUGS AND LESS
RIDICULOUS FACIAL HAIR.

UPGRADE: DESPITE BEING INJECTED WITH NANOBYTES, UNCLE MITCH HAD NO POWERS AND SPENT MUCH OF HIS TIME FLIRTING WITH SCIENCE TEAM MEMBERS AND SECURITY GUARDS. SHORTLY AFTER, HIS UPGRADES WERE REMOVED AND THE UPGRADE CHAIR WAS REPROGRAMMED SO THAT NO ADULT COULD RECEIVE NANOBYTES.

LEVEL 10
ACCESS GRANTED

BEGIN TRANSMISSION:

28

38°53' N, 77°1' W

When the time machine flashed into August 16, 1987, Miss Information realized that perhaps she should have entered more detailed information about exactly where in Washington, D.C., the machine should drop them. It occurred to her that they could have appeared right in the middle of traffic and been hit by a bus. But there was nothing barreling at them. In fact, there was nothing in the street at all except for a few parked cars. It seemed peculiar that a street in downtown Washington, D.C., during lunch hour would be so empty, but perhaps it was just her good luck. One thing was for sure: She had an incredible sense of déjà vu.

"Welcome to 1987, team. There's no Wi-Fi, no iPhones, no Facebook, and MTV still plays music videos," she said.

"What's a music video?" Tessa asked.

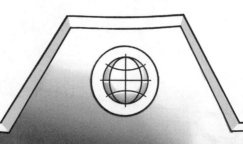

Miss Information frowned, suddenly feeling very old. "I hate you. I hate all of you."

She pressed a button on her time machine and watched it collapse into a small box.

She hefted Alex onto her back and pulled Benjy out of her pocket. The little robot floated next to her, buzzing and tweeting.

"Many of my functions are inoperable, including tele-communications. I've concluded that the satellites needed don't yet exist at this point in time."

"But you still have our list of targets, correct?" she said.

"I do. In fact, the first one should be along any moment."

Everyone peered down one end of the empty street, then they turned to peer down the other. No one was coming in either direction.

"You sure about that?" Tessa asked.

"I'm quite certain," Benjy said.

"Something's wrong," Miss Information said.

"Where are all the cars?" Snot Rocket asked.

"Benjy dear, what time is it, exactly?" Miss Information asked.

"Two thirty," he said.

"Two thirty in downtown D.C. You shouldn't be able to walk across this street, let alone stand in the middle of it for five minutes, without seeing so much as a kid on a bicycle."

"That's 'cause we redirected the traffic," a girl said as she stepped into the road. Miss Information recognized her at once. It was the poofy-haired kid with the superallergies—Ruby Peet. "There's a very important person on his way to the immigration office and we wanted to make sure he got there unharmed."

The migraine came on full force. Miss Information's brain felt like it was going to break in two. Was this real or was it a dream? She couldn't be certain. Whenever one of the NERDS showed up, she lost her focus. But why? "How did you find us?"

"We followed you," Ruby said. "You see, you weirdos have already been to this moment and you made a huge mess. You destroyed a bus, smashed a taxicab, and made a major blunder— you got your faces in the paper. That's the thing about wearing a black mask with a skull on it, lady. It draws a lot of attention."

A red-haired boy with glasses stepped next to her. Heathcliff! "It was easy to figure out that you had built a time machine, but we didn't know how to build one ourselves. That was until you made your second mistake. You shouldn't leave highly sensitive plans for time machines lying around your secret lair," he said. "Or leave a toxic trail to said secret lair that was easily tracked. Those are textbook no-no's for supervillains. Very sloppy work."

"But that wasn't your biggest mistake, Lisa," a man said as he joined the children in the road. He was wearing a tuxedo and using a cane. It was him—the man she dreamed about! But he wasn't supposed to be real . . . "Your biggest mistake was pretending to be someone that we could care about, because now you're surrounded by people who aren't ready to give up on you."

All of a sudden she couldn't stand. Her face felt like it was on fire, scorching her mind and cooking her memories, stirring them into some confusing stew. The name Alexander boomed in her thoughts. Alexander! She looked at her scarecrow boyfriend and then back at the stranger, trying to tell the two of them apart.

The man approached and tried to help her up, but she slashed his face with her fingernails, drawing blood. He fell back in surprise.

"Get away from me," she cried. "Whatever you think you've stopped, you're wrong. You're outnumbered. BULLIES!"

Her team circled her, ready to attack.

Five more children joined the trio. She had never seen any of them before, in dreams or in real life. They were a collection of runny-nosed losers holding some weird gadgets—clearly, no match for her BULLIES.

"Kill them!" Miss Information commanded.

Tessa raised her hands. "No!" she cried. "You didn't tell me I'd have to hurt anyone. I just wanted my dad's attention and I've made things worse. I can't get my dad back like this."

"Oh, Code Name to Be Decided, you disappoint me," Miss Information growled. "BULLIES, break some heads, starting with your leader."

The BULLIES assaulted everything that wasn't nailed down. Thor threw an uprooted tree at the NERDS, which missed and crashed into a building. The losers had to leap out of the way of Snot Rocket's mucus missiles, which blew up a parked car. Tammy's voice knocked over a phone booth that landed within a foot of Ruby Peet. Funk unleashed a dark cloud of body odor over the entire battle that caused everyone to double over, gagging.

Miss Information watched all the destruction admiringly. These kids were like artists who used violence instead of paint. They were incredible!

29

38°53' N, 77°1' W

Tessa was heartbroken. All this fighting and destruction, and for what? So her daddy would give her a hug? What had she been thinking? Now, here she was, a human target in the middle of an enormous battle. She had to escape. But how?

She scanned the road and quickly spotted her answer. The shiny silver time machine was lying on the sidewalk where Miss Information had dropped it. Ducking explosions, she ran to it and pressed the buttons just like she had seen her wicked boss do. It unfolded right before her eyes. The control panel dazzled with possibilities, but where should she go? And when? Was there some place in all of space and time that she could hide from Miss Information? Her heart sank. The answer was likely no. The woman was relentless, and it wouldn't be long before she'd be erasing Tessa, too.

If that were the case, she wanted a chance to say good-bye to her family.

She entered an address and a date, and with all her strength she turned the wheel to start the machine. It barely moved. She wasn't sure she was strong enough, but she had to be. Slowly but surely, with straining muscles and tears streaming down her cheeks, she turned the wheel faster and faster. Tessa Lipton vanished from the year 1987.

When the machine stopped, she stood outside Arlington Memorial Hospital. The readout said July 29, 2001. She pressed the button that shrank the time machine and shoved it in her pocket.

"Hi, I'm looking for someone who just had a baby," she told the receptionist.

"Are you family?"

Tessa smiled. "I am."

Moments later, she stood outside room 408, peering through the doorway at her mother and father. They looked so young. Her mom held a newborn girl in her arms. She looked exhausted. Her father was talking on a cell phone.

She checked the hall for prying eyes then transformed her face until it was a match for the receptionist's.

"Hello, Mr. and Mrs. Lipton," she said when she slipped into their room. "I hear congratulations are in order."

Her father waved her off, busy with his phone call. Her mother smiled. "This is my baby girl—meet Tessa."

Tessa smiled at herself. *Darn, I was cute*, she thought.

"You must be very proud."

"Oh, we are."

"Seems like your husband is a very busy man," she said.

"He is," her mother said. "He's running for mayor."

Her father held the phone to his chest and flashed his best smile. "I hope I can count on your vote."

"Well, I'm not so sure about that," Tessa said.

"Oh?"

"I hardly think I could vote for someone who puts his business before his family."

Her father's face turned pink with embarrassment. He looked at the phone and flipped it closed. "I feel like I'm going to get a lecture," he said sheepishly.

It was Tessa's turn to blush. She had to be careful. She didn't want to make her parents so mad they would ask to have her removed, especially since this might be the last time she ever saw them.

"What I mean is, a leader has to have time for his family."

"She's right!" her mother cried. "You have a brand-new baby girl and you're on the phone."

Tessa turned to her mother. "And don't you make excuses for him missing out on things, Mom—I mean, Mrs. Lipton—you have to put your foot down. This man is going to be the president some day and—"

"President?" her father said.

"Don't give him any big ideas," her mother said with a laugh, then turned to her husband. "She's right, you know. This little girl is going to need you. I don't want you to run for any office if the family has to suffer."

Her father thought for a long moment and then smiled. "All right. It's a deal," he said, taking the baby into his arms. "Now let me take a look at my little girl. She's a beauty. Just like her mom."

"She's going to love you like crazy," Tessa said as she opened the door.

"And the feeling will be mutual," her dad replied.

She congratulated them again, and closed the door behind her. When the coast was clear, she shifted her features back to her own. She smiled, happy that if she were to suddenly not exist that at least she would go knowing that once upon a time, the Liptons were a real family.

30

Despite the chaos around them,
Alexander approached Miss Information with open arms. "Lisa,
I can help you."

"My name is not Lisa," Miss Information said.

"Fine, Viktoriya. But I know you as Lisa Holiday," he said.

Viktoriya. Why did that name seem familiar? And Lisa
Holiday? Where had she heard that name before? Wait—Lisa
was a librarian. She wore cardigan sweaters and baked cookies.
She took care of some very special kids and she was in love with
a spy. *She* was Lisa.

NO! SHE WAS MISS INFORMATION.

The NERDS charged. One of the kids shot Thor with a
lightning bolt, another built an enormous net out of macramé
and tangled Loudmouth inside it. A small, frail girl vanished

right before her eyes, and seconds later a floating piece of lumber hit Snot Rocket in the nose. Another kid fired lasers from his eyes, and yet another snatched Funk by the collar and rose on stilts four stories into the air.

The strange man continued toward her. "I know about your past. I know about the spying and the villain virus. I also know that you've gone through something that no person could handle. You're not well, but I can help."

"I don't need your help," she shouted. "And you don't know me!"

The headache came back, and without warning she reeled

back like a cobra protecting her nest. With a sudden, forceful punch, she hit the man on the side of his head. He fell to the ground and lay still.

"Benjy, where did I put my time machine?"

"I observed Ms. Lipton stealing it several minutes ago. I'm afraid it is gone," the orb clicked.

"Oh, poo!" she said. "Wait! How did this man get here?"

The orb spun around in midair. "My sensors are detecting trace elements of temporal radiation within twenty yards," it said. "It could be used in a time travel device."

"Benjy? Do you see that up ahead in the middle of the road?"

"It appears to be a pool of colored plastic balls," the robot said. "The nuclear signature is emanating from it."

Miss Information smiled. "Benjy, do you have a date for Ms. Peet?"

"June 14, 1996. On that day, Francis Peet and his fiancée, Sarah Kaplan, married in a beach community called Fair Harbor, part of the Fire Island region of Long Island."

"Let's go crash a wedding!"

END TRANSMISSION.

TOP SECRET DOSSIER
CODE NAME: DUDEBOT
REAL NAME: 45X ATTACK DROID
ACTIVE: 1987
CURRENT OCCUPATION:
DEACTIVATED

HISTORY: 45X WAS THE CREATION OF THE EVIL MASTERMIND HENRY SINISTER. IT MALFUNCTIONED DURING A BATTLE WITH THE NERDS IN 1987. WHILE ATTEMPTING TO REACTIVATE ITS MEMORY BANK, AGENT BOOKWORM SPILLED A BOTTLE OF HAWAIIAN PUNCH INTO ITS CIRUITS AND THE FORMER KILLER ROBOT BECOME DUDEBOT, THE PARTY DROID. DUDEBOT LOVED ALL THINGS SUN, SURF, AND SIESTA AND WAS KNOWN FOR LISTENING TO JIMMY BUFFETT RECORDS NONSTOP. THAT, COUPLED WITH HIS ENDLESS USE OF "DUDE," "BRO," AND "PARTY ON!" EVENTUALLY ANNOYED HIS TEAMMATES, WHO DEACTIVATED HIM WITH A BASEBALL BAT.

UPGRADE: OTHER THAN HIS ABILITY
TO ANNOY PEOPLE WITH HIS STUPID
CATCHPHRASES AND SINGING OF
THE SONG "CHEESEBURGER IN
PARADISE," DUDEBOT HAD
NO REAL POWERS.

LEVEL 11
ACCESS GRANTED

BEGIN TRANSMISSION:

31

38°53' N, 77°1' W

Ruby watched as the BULLIES retreated. Luckily, they'd backed off just as the NERDS were about to lose the fight. Her team from 1977 hooted and hollered. They had their first mission under their belts. She found Heathcliff in the crowd, and together they located Agent Brand, who was lying on the ground, unconscious. The children shook him until his eyes opened and then helped him to his feet.

"That woman's got a serious left hook," he said, rubbing his temple.

"She knocked you out again? This is starting to become a habit," Ruby said.

Brand frowned. "Where'd they go?"

"I have a bad feeling she went *there*," Heathcliff said, pointing toward their time machine.

"That's not good!" Ruby shouted as she tore off toward the pit. The NERDS and Heathcliff sprinted after her.

"I'm sorry," Rupert cried. "Those weirdos just got up and ran off. I thought they were trying to save themselves from more butt-kicking. I didn't think they were going to use our time machine."

"It's not your fault. You guys did a great job," Brand said.

"Where do you think they went?" Ruby asked as Heathcliff pressed buttons on the control panel.

"According to the log they went to some beach on Long Island," Heathcliff said.

Ruby grabbed him by the collar. "What day?"

"June 14, 1996."

Ruby felt like someone had just sucker punched her in the gut. "That's the day my parents got married! She's going to try and stop the wedding."

"Let's go," Brand said. He snatched the controls from Heathcliff, pressed some buttons, and leaped into the pit. A second later he was gone.

"We'll go with you, too," Rupert said.

"No," Ruby said. "If they beat us, they'll come for you next. Go back to your time and get ready for her to show up. If she stops you, the NERDS will never happen."

"Do you think we're ready?" Static Cling asked.

Ruby nodded. "More than ready."

Heathcliff climbed into the pit. "Pretty awesome to meet you," he said to the NERDS, then sank below the balls. Ruby was next.

"Good luck," Rupert said.

"You too," Ruby said as she vanished from 1987.

She found Heathcliff and Agent Brand waiting for her on a wooden dock that looked out over a bay. There was a small receiving building, a tiny fire station, and a playground in the distance. A couple kids on bicycles raced each other, and the sky was a dark gray with low-hanging clouds threatening rain.

"Have you seen them?" she asked.

Brand shook his head. "No sign of them at all."

Heathcliff turned to one of the kids on a bike. "Hey, did you see a woman in a skull mask and four kids come past here?"

The kid screeched to a halt. "Hard to miss! They were headed for the beach."

He pointed down a pathway in between some cottages and dense patches of trees.

"C'mon," Ruby said, rushing down the path, which was nothing more than wooden planks stuck in the sand. The houses that lined the boardwalk were quaint summer rentals with names like Ferryport Landing and Land Ho! Her parents often talked about Fair Harbor. It was one of her family's favorite vacation places. Her home was lined with pictures of them on the beach, building drip castles, and eating lactose-free ice cream cones.

The island was less than three-quarters of a mile wide so Ruby, Heathcliff, and Brand soon arrived at a sandy beach. The salty Atlantic air pinched Ruby's nose and the crash of the surf filled her ears. Not more than ten yards away stood her mother and father, both young, and wildly in love. Sarah wore a long lacy white dress and had flowers in her hair. Her father was in an old-fashioned three-button suit and had his pant legs rolled up to his knees. Neither of them wore shoes. They were surrounded by family. She spotted Grandpa Saul, Aunt Laura, Uncle Eddie, Uncle Jeff, and the rest. There were no chairs, so they gathered around the happy couple while a man in a white suit read passages from a book titled *The Velveteen Rabbit*. Oddly enough, no one was arguing. In fact, she saw smiles on all of their faces. Her big, chaotic, bickering family was actually getting along.

"Where is she?" Heathcliff whispered.

"I have no idea," Brand said.

"What's the plan?" Heathcliff asked.

"Let's mingle," Ruby said. "If the BULLIES attack, at least we'll be where the action is."

The trio crept onto the beach and joined the crowd, smiling at people and acting as if they belonged.

"Sarah Kaplan, do you, before friends and family, give

yourself to this man, Francis Peet, to be his lawfully wedded wife as witnessed by this gathering and heaven above?"

Sarah's smile was blinding. "I do."

"Francis Peet, do you, before friends and family, give yourself to this woman, Sarah Kaplan, to be her lawfully wedded husband as witnessed by this gathering and heaven above?"

Francis nodded. "I do."

"And now by the powers vested in me, I declare this man and this woman lawfully—"

"Now, now, let's not get ahead of ourselves," said a voice from behind the group. Ruby's heart sank. It was Miss Information.

Everyone turned to see who had caused the ruckus, and a collective gasp erupted from the crowd when they saw her mask and gang of misfits. The scarecrow in the tuxedo didn't help, either.

"Isn't there supposed to be a part where you ask if anyone objects?" Miss Information said. "'Cause I really do object."

"Listen, lady, this is a private function," Grandma Rose said. "So why don't you take it down the beach?"

"Yeah, what kind of lunatic just walks up to a wedding and causes trouble?" Aunt Suzi shouted.

"Are you crazy?" Uncle Kevin cried.

"I'M NOT CRAZY!" Miss Information roared.

Ruby, Brand, and Heathcliff stepped forward.

"These people are innocent," Ruby said, looking straight at Miss Information. "I'm not going to let you hurt them."

"Hey, kid, thanks for the help, but we don't need it. No one messes with the Peet family," Uncle Eddie shouted. "We're from Boston!"

"Or the Kaplans," Grandma Tina cried, "representing Long Island!"

"Your feeble posturing doesn't impress me, folks," Miss Information said. "Unless you people want to get hurt, I suggest you call this wedding off and go home."

"Get her!" Grandpa Saul shouted.

Much to Ruby's surprise, the entire wedding party rushed at Miss Information and the goons. They tossed full bottles of wine and swatted at the intruders with umbrellas. Grandma Rose beat Snot Rocket with one of her shoes. Uncle Jeff shoved a bouquet of flowers into Funk's mouth. Miss Information backed toward the surf, dodging flying plates and trays of cookies.

"Do you think you can come here and cause trouble and get away with it?" Aunt Delynn shouted.

Just when things couldn't get worse for the thugs, the sky opened up and rain fell down in sheets, soaking everyone but not quenching the family's anger. In the storm, the villains stumbled back. Thor slipped and fell in the wet sand.

"Well, I have to admit, I didn't see this coming," Ruby said as she stood back and watched the mob attack their enemy.

"I don't know who the world has to fear more: Miss Information or your family," Heathcliff said.

Miss Information tried to dodge a flying purse. As she struggled to stay upright, she accidentally dropped Alex, and the waves dragged the scarecrow out to sea.

"Alex!" she cried. "Don't leave me! What use is ruling the world without the man I love by my side?"

The strange dummy sank beneath the water and disappeared.

Snot Rocket whined, "I can't see a foot in front of me."

Aunt Laura hit him with a bouquet of flowers, followed by an enthusiastic punch.

"What are we doing here?" Funk asked Miss Information. "Are you just sending us from one time to the next so we can feel what it's like to get beaten up in different eras?"

Thor grunted angrily.

"You ungrateful little toads!" Miss Information said, fighting off Grandma Tina. "I turned you kids into gods, and you haven't stopped boohooing for a second. When we get back, you're all going into the tiger cage."

"Then I quit!" Loudmouth shouted, and without a word she jumped into the ball pit and vanished.

Ruby was soaked, and her wet, poofy hair fell into her eyes. "Heathcliff, I can't see a thing. What's happening?"

"They're all abandoning her," Brand replied. "I just saw Snot Rocket and Funk use the time machine. Heathcliff, you need to stop them. Ruby and I will stay here and stop Lisa."

"Um, reminder here! I don't have any powers," Heathcliff cried.

"But you're one of *us*," Ruby said. "Do the best you can!"

Heathcliff took a moment to muster all his courage, and then he sprinted through the mob and leaped into the ball pit.

Miss Information stood her ground. "Benjy, how about a hand?" she shouted.

"I'm afraid I do not have hands," Benjy said. "But I will do my best."

The little orb darted into action, floating above the crowd and firing tiny blasts of electricity at everyone.

"Why would she do this?" Sarah cried into Francis's arms. "She ruined everything."

"No, she hasn't," Ruby said to her mother. "If you want to be in this family, you have to have an appetite for chaos."

Francis laughed. "You know—she's right."

Sarah grinned. "I'm sorry, but do we know you?"

"Not yet," Ruby said.

"C'mon," Brand shouted. He raced into the crowd and Ruby followed. She watched as he got beneath the robot orb Miss Information called Benjy. He swung his cane at it, attracting two nasty bolts of electricity just before he connected. When it fell into the sand, he stomped on it, cracking it into three pieces. The purple light faded.

"Nice shot, boss," Ruby said.

"Yeah, did you ever play any baseball?"

Ruby turned to see who owned the voice and found Jackson, Matilda, Flinch, and Duncan standing behind her.

"You're back!" she said, pulling them all into a group hug.

"I'm not sure what you're talking about, but I'm pretty sure this hug is weird," Matilda said.

"We'll explain later," Brand said. He pointed at Miss Information, who was crawling into the ball pit and disappearing. "She's given up on you, Ruby, but she's off to cause trouble somewhere else."

"We've got to go after her," Matilda said. "It feels like I haven't socked someone in the jaw in like forever."

"No. Heathcliff needs you. Figure out where he went and stop the BULLIES," Brand commanded as he walked to the pit. "I'll go after her."

"But—" Ruby said.

"That's an order," Brand said as he climbed into the time machine. A moment later he was gone.

32

38°46' N, 77°4' W

"What are we doing back here?"
Funk asked as Snot Rocket led them through the empty
corridors of Miss Information's lair.

"It's a week before we first left the time stream. The boss
abandoned us, Tessa betrayed us, and I'm tired of getting my
butt kicked by a bunch of nerds. If they come looking for us,
they're going to regret it," Snot Rocket cried.

When they got to the upgrade room, he pressed the
button to open the door and dragged the others inside with
him. A moment later, the door closed and a bank of laser
lights scanned their bodies.

"Didn't we already do this?" Loudmouth cried. "It hurt
like the dickens."

"We're doing it again. If it made us strong the first time,

imagine what it will do to us when we go back for seconds," Snot Rocket said. "We'll be unstoppable."

"SCANNING FOR STRENGTHS," an electronic voice said. **"ENHANCEMENTS AVAILABLE INITIATE UPGRADE?"**

"Do your worst!" Funk shouted.

The needles and tubes dropped down around them.

33

Heathcliff emerged from the ball
pit inside Miss Information's lair. He figured by now there
must be ball pits all over the timeline. He'd have to remember
to deactivate them all when he returned to his original time.
If he returned. He hoped Ruby and Brand would come find
him when they were finished with their timeline. It would be
no fun living a life where he was a week behind himself.

He heard the BULLIES' footsteps echoing down a hall
and so he followed them, catching up just as they entered
the upgrade room. The metal door closed tight, sealing them
inside. He shuddered at what he knew was coming next.
Upgrade rooms granted incredible powers. No one, however,
had ever gotten a double dose of nanobytes. He dreaded
finding out how it would change the BULLIES. He also knew

there was nothing he could do to stop them. The door was locked, and even shutting off the power wouldn't stop the upgrade process.

So he waited, and tried to come up with a plan. How was he, the shrimpiest of the agents, with zero powers, going to stop four hulking freaks? And then it dawned on him. If Miss Information's secret lair was just like the Playground, there had to be gadgets in the science lab. He dashed through the halls, past the control room, and into the science center. Racing up and down, he eyed one dangerous-looking contraption after another.

He grabbed what looked like a laser gun from a low-budget space movie. He had no idea what it did, so he aimed it at the wall and fired. A second later everything in the laser's path was encased in a thick layer of ice.

"This could come in handy," he said, taking off his backpack and unzipping it. He planned on stuffing it with the laser and anything else that would fit inside, but his eye caught something silver.

Benjamin! *He* would know what to do. The orb had been the greatest ally the NERDS ever had.

Carefully, Heathcliff laid out the pieces of the broken orb. Then he got to work. It wasn't long before the charred copper wires were gone and fresh ones had taken their place. He double-checked his work, not wanting to repeat the tragedy of his last attempt. Then, he snapped the two sides together and pressed the on button.

As before, the ball glowed red before it turned blue. Spinning around on the table, it clicked and beeped, finally rising upward until it was inches from Heathcliff's face.

"Benjamin?"

"Heathcliff Hodges," it replied. There was something tentative in its voice. "I'm having some difficulty accessing my satellite link. I need to reboot for time and date and hop onto the data stream—"

"Don't do anything unnecessary, Benjamin," Heathcliff said. "We could mess up your internal programming. We've gone back in time."

"I see . . . ," the robot said with even more hesitation.

"I'm so happy you're back! You were damaged by Ms. Holiday," he said. "I'll explain more later, but right now we have a bigger problem. There are a bunch of thugs inside an upgrade room and they're getting a massive dose of nanobytes. I have no idea how to stop them. I'm powerless and—"

Suddenly, Benjamin was zipping around Heathcliff's head like an angry hornet. "I suppose this is part of another one of your diabolical schemes."

"No, I—"

"You might be able to fool the others, but I've been around a long time, kid."

Heathcliff's heart sank. "What did I do?"

"Huh?"

"I have no memories of the year and a half before I woke up in the Playground. No one will tell me anything. I know it's bad, Benjamin, but I have a right to know."

The orb spun around and clicked. "Heathcliff, is this some kind of trick?"

Heathcliff shook his head. "The last thing I remember was Jackson joining the team. *You* know what happened, don't you?"

"An analysis of your heartbeat indicates that you are telling the truth."

Heathcliff wiped away tears and nodded his head. "I am."

"Are you sure you want to know?"

Heathcliff nodded.

"Very well," the orb said as light shot out and swirled around Heathcliff in a three-dimensional projection.

He saw himself putting on a black mask with a white skull— exactly like the one Ms. Holiday was now wearing. He saw a machine on a patch of ice at the North Pole. He saw it rising up into the sky, creating a monstrous mountain. He saw himself falling into the water. He saw himself running through the streets of Washington followed by an army of squirrels. He saw himself threatening a large fat man who later transformed himself into a living machine. Then he saw himself in group therapy with several other costumed people. He saw himself blackmail Ruby when she came to him for help. He saw himself stepping into another world and sitting in an upgrade chair and turning himself into an enormous head—a freakish monster that could wipe away the world with a single thought. Then he saw himself sedated and unconscious, attached to tubes, as Flinch shrank himself so he could be injected into Heathcliff's brain. He saw the horror. He saw the fear. He saw the chaos. He saw the insanity.

The projection stopped, but his head was ablaze. Every moment, feeling, and dark plan of the last year and a half wrestled for his immediate attention. It was too much. He screamed out in pain.

He must have passed out because he woke on the floor with Benjamin's voice asking if he was OK. He stood up, dusted off his clothes, and ran a tongue over the false teeth that had been inserted where his real teeth once were.

"I'm great, Benjamin. I actually feel like my old self again."

He snatched the ball in midair and raced out of the room, down the hall, toward the exit tubes.

"Heathcliff, I'm sensing disturbing sounds coming from this place's upgrade room. Shouldn't we investigate?"

"There's no time," he said.

"Why?"

"Because, you stupid wad of aluminum foil, I'm going to take over the world!" he cried.

END TRANSMISSION.

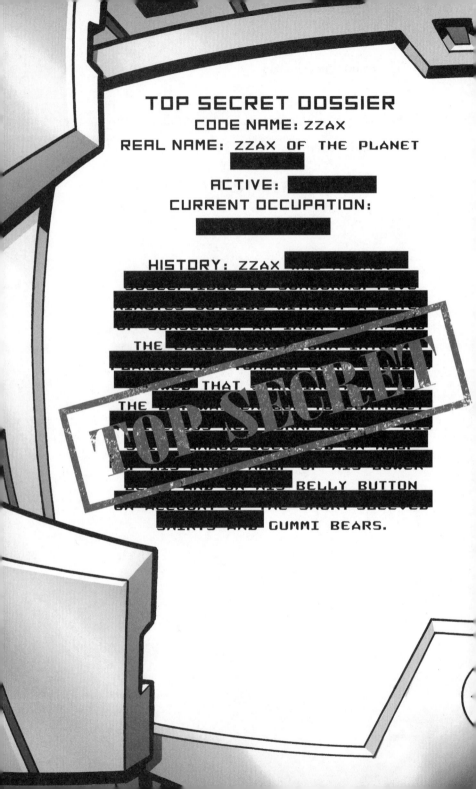

TOP SECRET DOSSIER
CODE NAME: ZZAX
REAL NAME: ZZAX OF THE PLANET ▮▮▮▮▮

ACTIVE: ▮▮▮▮▮▮

CURRENT OCCUPATION: ▮▮▮▮▮▮

HISTORY: ZZAX ▮▮▮▮▮▮▮▮▮ ▮▮▮▮▮▮▮▮▮▮▮▮▮▮▮▮ THE ▮▮▮▮▮▮▮▮▮▮▮ ▮▮▮▮▮▮ THAT ▮▮▮▮▮▮▮ THE ▮▮▮▮▮▮▮▮▮▮▮ ▮▮▮▮▮▮▮▮▮▮▮ ▮▮▮▮▮▮▮▮ BELLY BUTTON ▮▮▮▮▮▮▮▮▮▮ ▮▮▮ GUMMI BEARS.

LEVEL 12
ACCESS GRANTED

BEGIN TRANSMISSION:

34

Heathcliff floated down the entrance tube and landed on the floor of the deserted Playground. Because he'd arrived a week in the past to follow the BULLIES, the Playground hadn't been destroyed yet.

Benjamin squirmed in his hand but could not break free from his grip. "Heathcliff, don't do this," the orb begged. "Don't abuse your team's trust again."

Heathcliff ignored the plea and marched to the upgrade room. Once inside, he activated the process while his mind lit up with possibilities. What kind of power would he have this time, and how would it be useful for taking over the world? Would it help him seek revenge on the people he once called friends—the ones who had lied to him for months?

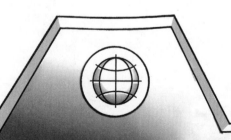

"SCANNING FOR WEAKNESSES."

The lasers danced over him. The psychic powers he had before had been delicious. If only he could get them once more. He wouldn't mind the hypnotic teeth, either. Those were cool.

"SUBJECT HAS SUPERIOR INTELLECT AND IS IN GOOD PHYSICAL HEALTH CONSIDERING COMPLETE LACK OF EXERCISE," the computer said.

"What's wrong? Don't tell me I am perfect! You have to find something, no matter how small."

"WEAKNESS DETECTED," the computer said. **"PREPARE FOR UPGRADE."**

Tubes and needles dropped from the ceiling and hovered above his body. A platform rose below him and forced him flat on his back. A second later his arms and legs were strapped down.

"What is it? What's my weakness?"

"SUBJECT NEEDS HIS PARENTS," the machine said.

"What?"

"ONLY PARENTS CAN STEER YOU TOWARD A HAPPY LIFE UPGRADING NOW."

"How is that going to help me take over the world?" he shouted, but the machine did not respond.

The needles injected him with nanobytes and he winced in pain. "Benjamin! Get me out of this," he begged.

"Sorry, Hodges. But if it makes you feel any better, I would have thought you needed a spanking," Benjamin said.

Heathcliff watched as the tiny black robots swirled down a tube and into a needle inserted in his hand. And then everything went black.

"You're alone, Hodges," a voice said to Heathcliff. He was standing in complete darkness and couldn't even see his hand in front of his face. "Always alone. Who do you think is to blame?"

Heathcliff snarled. "I don't need a lecture."

"There is no one in the world who needs a lecture more than you. Look around. You have no family. No friends. How did this happen?"

"Go away!"

"It was your anger. You might have been someone great, but you squandered it on rage."

"Blah! Blah! Blah!"

Suddenly, Heathcliff found himself seated in a movie theater and the screen was alight with images of his future. He was happy. He was married with a little boy of his own, and he was teaching him about science and his favorite comic book characters. He had a great job, helping people at a laboratory that made medicine, and every night he went home, had dinner with his family, and laughed.

The movie stopped, and when the lights came on he was surprised to see himself sitting next to him, and even more surprised to see that it was a version of him with his old enormous buckteeth.

"You gave that up," the figure said. "You can't blame the bullies for what has happened. You can't blame Jackson Jones. You decided on this path. Does it make you happy?"

Heathcliff turned to his double. "No, it doesn't but what can I do? I'm evil."

"You stop."

"Just stop?"

The boy nodded.

"Just stop. You have more important things to do, you know. It's time to use that big brain for something good. Go save the world."

Heathcliff woke with a gasp. Benjamin was hovering over him, zipping and shaking.

"If you move, I'll blast you, kid," he chirped.

"Want to help me save the world?"

Benjamin spun around but said nothing for a long moment. "Seriously?"

"C'mon!" Heathcliff cried. He darted out of the upgrade room. He raced down the hall and into the control center. "Benjamin, I need to see what our BULLIES are up to."

A huge screen dropped from above and blinked to life. A TV news anchor stood in front of the school while the BULLIES—each one of them nearly three stories tall, attacked the building. Whatever they had done in the upgrade room had turned them into giants.

"OK, that's not good," he said. "All right, think. I'm the only member of the team in this time stream and my upgrades . . . no upgrades. There are four monsters attacking our school. Any suggestions?"

"We need more agents," Benjamin said. "Should we call in some veterans?"

Heathcliff shook his head. "It would take them too long to get here and most of them are too old for the upgrade chair. What I need are some new recruits. But where . . ." He looked upward.

"Heathcliff?" Benjamin said with more than a little worry in his robotic voice, but Heathcliff was already racing toward the exit tubes.

He slammed a button on the podium and a second later he and Benjamin were sucked up into the lockers of Thomas Knowlton Middle School. Heathcliff blasted through the tiny door and into an empty hallway.

"Where is everybody?"

"My sensors are detecting a rather pungent smell," Benjamin said.

"It's called lunch," Heathcliff said.

He ran down the hall and shoved open the double doors that led to the school cafeteria. His arrival was so loud that everyone turned to him.

"My name is Heathcliff Hodges and I'm a spy. Who wants superpowers?"

The kids looked at him as if he were one flapjack short of a stack.

"A little help here, Benjamin?" he begged.

The robot zipped around the room projecting images of Flinch, Pufferfish, Braceface, Gluestick, Wheezer, and Choppers fighting bad guys. "He's telling the truth."

All at once, every kid in the school jumped out of their seat and collectively shouted, "I do!"

"Follow me!" Heathcliff cried.

He ran back down the hall and threw his locker door open, shoving kids in one by one.

"Just to be clear, I think this is a terrible idea," Benjamin said.

Heathcliff smiled. "Benjamin, this is the best idea I have ever had."

35

Brand was very unhappy with where and when the time machine had taken him—Nathan Hale Elementary, May 1976. The school was still a construction site. Metal beams hung overhead and huge industrial machines were parked nearby. In a year, the school would open, and the NERDS would be born. But on this day there were no agents, no gadgets, and no fellow spies to help him stop Lisa Holiday.

"You're too late," she said. She was standing nearby with a sledgehammer resting on her shoulder.

"Am I?" Brand asked. "What is it you plan on doing?"

"Why, I'm going to destroy this site. I may not be able to erase your precious NERDS agents, but I can still make sure the organization was never born." She swung the heavy hammer at him. He barely had time to step out of its way.

"Why are you here?" she asked.

"Because I love you," he said.

"And you think you can help me? So one day I'll be better and you and I can . . . what? Get married? Have a family? Buy a house with a little picket fence and save the world on the weekends? That's never going to happen, and it's not because I'm so bad and you're so good. It's because I don't care about you. I never cared about you. You were an assignment and I manipulated you."

"I don't believe that."

She laughed. "You're a fool. Do you know how many men I've done this to? You're not special."

The words stung him, but he kept moving toward her. "Even with that mask on, I can see you're lying. You aren't bad. You aren't Miss Information. You're a librarian who works at a school full of superpowered kids and you bake lousy deserts and worry too much."

Miss Information buckled over in pain.

"Lisa!"

"These headaches! They confuse me," she said. Her bitter tone was gone.

"It's your mind rebelling against what you've become," Brand said. "Let it go, Lisa. Let all of this go."

"Alex? Please help me, Alex. I'm so confused."

She reached up and removed her mask. There was the face that made him smile—the face that smoothed his rough edges—but she was in so much pain.

"It's going to be OK," he said, taking her into his arms.

He felt her jerk. Instinctively, he snatched her hand. There was a pipe in it.

"I almost got you!" she said with a wicked grin. She swung at him with her fists and he hobbled out of her reach. She leaped into the air with a foot aimed at his neck, but he batted it away and stepped to the side, grabbing the back of her hair and slamming her to the ground.

She hopped to her feet with unexpected agility and karate-chopped his belly. He bent over in agony and fell to avoid another kick, rolling away just as she stomped heeled boots where his neck had been. One boot got so close he had to catch it in his hands before it crushed his windpipe. He fought hard against it, thrusting upward and causing her to do a backflip in midair. She landed safely, but she was far enough away from him so that he had time to stand. He grabbed his cane and waved it at her.

"Is that all you've got?" he said.

The taunt sent her charging forward, but when she was close enough, he used the cane to catch her foot. A strong jerk and she was flat on her face. By the growl she let loose he could tell she was frustrated. *Yes, get mad. Then you'll make mistakes.*

"Lisa—"

"STOP CALLING ME THAT!" she shrieked, racing at him like a runaway train. Her punches were fast and her feet faster. He blocked every attack, but each blow took more and more out of him. She pushed him backward, step-by-step, and finally he lost his footing, falling over a bag of concrete and slamming his head hard on a monkey wrench that was lying on the ground. He tried to stand, but his legs would not cooperate.

Miss Information grabbed a handful of electrical wiring and went to the time machine. She dipped one end of the wire into the ball pit and connected the second to the control panel. At once, a shrieking sound filled the air.

"Your little time machine is nothing more than a wormhole expander. I set it up to tear one into a ragged wound. The result will be a very big bang, sweetie. Once the battery cells overload, it will vaporize this site and stop your headquarters from ever existing."

Brand cursed his body. Why couldn't he stand? "Sort of defeats the purpose. If you're caught in the blast, how will you rule the world? That's what you want, right?"

She shook her head. "Oh, I'll be long gone before then." She pushed a couple of buttons and stepped into the pit, then turned and blew him a kiss. "Don't look so sad. I think Lisa did love you. If only she were real."

With what little strength he had, he snatched the monkey wrench and threw it. It slammed into the ball pit's control panel. Sparks and black smoke filled the air, and the screeching noise got louder and higher in pitch.

The woman screamed in terror. "You've reversed the engine! You've created a black hole. It's going to crush me!"

Brand crawled on his hands and knees to reach her. "Take my hand!" he cried, but she couldn't move from the ball pit. A terrible, crackling energy rose up out of the machine and engulfed her body. She shook in pain.

"Lisa!"

"Alex, I wanted to tell you who I was, but I didn't really know."

"You're Lisa Holiday," he cried.

"I wanted to be," she said.

There was a massive shock wave and Ms. Holiday's body broke into a million tiny flecks of dust. They rose up into the air like dandelion seeds on a summer breeze and drifted over the entire construction site. All that remained was the black mask with the white skull painted on it.

Brand staggered to his feet and approached the ball pit. He gave the control panel a shake. It popped on and off. He pressed some buttons, made a wish, then crawled into the ball pit once more. It might kill him, too, but he had to try.

36

38°46' N, 77°4' W

"No one can stop us!" the thirty-foot-tall Snot Rocket cried. He stomped through the streets, snapping electrical wires with every step. He fired a massive booger at a car. It exploded. The other BULLIES cheered. Each one was as big as Snot Rocket.

Loudmouth opened her mouth and a tornado blasted out of her lungs, ripping apart the street, tearing the roof off a nearby home, and pushing a garage off its foundation.

Thor roared and beat on his chest. His protruding veins were thick with boiling purple blood and his eyes were bulging.

"Anything we want is ours!" Funk shouted. His armpit smell caused a mailbox to ignite and melt. "And no one can stop us!"

"Um, excuse me," Heathcliff said from far below.

Snot Rocket looked down at the little boy. He was standing in front of a sea of other puny children.

"We've come to stop you," Heathcliff said. He hoped that the giants wouldn't stomp on him right away.

"Are you sure this is going to work, Hodges?" Benjamin asked. "I don't want to end up in a recycling bin."

"I don't know," Heathcliff admitted. "I've never confronted four superpowered giants before."

"You're one of those NERDS," Funk said, his voice booming like thunder. "The one without any powers. What did you do, kid, gather up your weakling friends to come out here and give us a piece of your mind?"

"Not exactly," Heathcliff said. He turned to his army. *"Get them!"*

All at once, three hundred once-average kids attacked. Their weaknesses had been enhanced by nanobytes. Some of them could fly, some were very strong, and others were as fast as lightning. One kid could bounce like a basketball—he slammed into Funk's face. Another turned to ice and blasted Tammy's shoes until she hopped around with frozen toes. One kid turned into a hairy beast and attacked Snot Rocket with claws and teeth, and another kid produced so much sweat it caused Thor to slip and fall on his back. There were kids who teleported and kids who could move objects with their thoughts. There were kids whose skin was as hard as rocks and others who turned into water and still others who were now half cyborg. And together they were led by Heathcliff Hodges.

"It's working!" Heathcliff cried.

But he spoke too soon. With a massive swipe of his paw, Thor knocked fifty of the children unconscious.

"Get back!" Heathcliff shouted, but it was too late.

Funk unleashed his powers, bringing a thousand enormous maggots from underground. They slithered over more of the would-be heroes.

It sent a panic through Heathcliff's army. A few hurt themselves trying to retaliate. Others had no idea how to use their nanobytes in the first place. Heathcliff had gambled and lost. Unfortunately, it appeared the world had lost, too.

"You look like you need some help, pal," Jackson said. Heathcliff turned in time to see the boy climb out of a ball pit that had materialized behind him. Duncan, Flinch, Matilda, and Ruby were next.

"So, I see you've been busy," Ruby said.

"Desperate times," he said.

"He's been doing a good job," Benjamin beeped.

"You're back!" Duncan cried.

"Mr. Hodges fixed me," the orb said. "It's very good to see you all, again. However, might we save our reunion for another time? When we're not playing Jack to these giants?"

Ruby started scratching her legs. "Aargh! I'm allergic to end-of-the-world scenarios."

"So, what's the plan?" Heathcliff said to her. She smiled. He knew she liked running the show, even when the show looked like it was going to end very badly.

"Matilda, fly up and blast Thor in the eyes with your inhalers. He can't hit what he can't see."

Matilda soared into the sky. A moment later she was zapping the angry beast in the face.

Ruby turned to Duncan. "How do you feel about being tossed in the air at a giant's face?"

"Um, OK . . . I guess," he said.

"Jackson, I need some of your quarterback skills. Toss Duncan at Loudmouth. Duncan, you need to seal her mouth tight with your glue."

"Excellent. And when I come falling out of the sky . . . ?"

"Flinch will be there to catch you," Ruby replied.

"I'm on it," Flinch said, shoving four Twinkies into his mouth. His body began to shake and he pounded on his chest. "I AM MIGHTY!"

"Good, cause when he's safe on the ground, I need you to target Funk," she said. "You're a lot faster than his nasty powers. I have a feeling you might be able to get him to accidentally turn his own grossness on himself."

"Yay!" Flinch cried as he swallowed a bag of Swedish Fish without chewing.

Jackson picked Duncan up with his braces. "You ready, pal?"

"Is anyone ever ready for something like this?" the boy asked.

Jackson aimed and threw. A second later, Flinch flashed through the mob to wait for his falling buddy.

"Do I get to do anything else?" Jackson asked.

"I think we could stop Snot Rocket if he had a bloody nose," Ruby answered with a grin.

Jackson winked. "Got a new trick I've been wanting to try out."

His braces poured out of his mouth, forming a massive exoskeleton as big as any of the BULLIES. Jackson sat in its center, looking like a massive Rock'em Sock'em Robot stomping toward Snot Rocket.

"I suppose you want me to hide," Heathcliff said. "I know I don't have any useful upgrades. I don't want to get in the way."

"Hodges, you have three hundred superpowered kids at your disposal," she said. "That's your army. When these jerks get knocked off their feet, we're going to need a whole bunch of them for wedgie duty."

There was a massive thud. Ruby and Heathcliff turned and saw that Thor had fallen onto his back.

"Kids, get him!" Heathcliff shouted, and he led his army into the fray. His team kicked and punched Thor and tied him to the ground.

Heathcliff cheered anew when each of the four horrific BULLIES fell. Being a part of the team—even if he couldn't do anything himself—was one of the most satisfying days of his life.

END TRANSMISSION.

TOP SECRET DOSSIER

CODE NAME: BEANPOLE
REAL NAME: MIKEY BUCKLEY
YEARS ACTIVE: 1977–82
CURRENT OCCUPATION:
CHILDREN'S BOOK AUTHOR,
NERDS CONSULTANT

HISTORY: IF ONE COULD SUM UP
THE MANY TALENTS AND GIFTS MIKEY
BUCKLEY POSSESSES IN A SINGLE WORD,
IT WOULD HAVE TO BE "BRILLIANT."
A RARE GENIUS WITH AN UNRIVALED
IMAGINATION, BEANPOLE IS BELIEVED
TO BE THE CREATOR OF THE BENJAMIN
ORB, THE UPGRADE CHAIR, FRENCH TOAST
STICKS, AND THE MOON BOOT STILTS
THAT ALLOWED HIM TO RISE NEARLY
FIVE STORIES ABOVE THE GROUND. I
COULD LITERALLY GO ON AND ON ABOUT
HOW COOL THAT KID WAS . . . AND HE
WAS GOOD-LOOKING, TO BOOT. BUT WHAT
COULD I SAY THAT HASN'T BEEN
SAID IN THE THOUSANDS OF
BIOGRAPHIES WRITTEN ABOUT
HIM, OR THE FOUR FEATURE
FILMS THAT ALL WON
OSCARS, OR THE ALBUMS
OF SONGS BY NIRVANA,

MADONNA, AND TAYLOR SWIFT
THAT HE INSPIRED? I MEAN, IF
YOU HAVEN'T READ THE BOOKS OF
POETRY ABOUT HIS HAIR ALONE,
THEN YOU'VE BEEN LIVING UNDER
A ROCK. SO, SUFFICE TO SAY,
BEANPOLE WAS THE GREATEST AGENT
IN NERDS HISTORY.

UPGRADE: WHAT COULD TECHNOLOGY
GIVE HIM THAT THE GOOD LORD HAD
NOT GENEROUSLY BESTOWED? THE
BOY WAS SIMPLY AWESOME!

LEVEL 13
ACCESS GRANTED

BEGIN TRANSMISSION:

37

38°52' N, 77°6' W

When the NERDS used the ball pit
to return to the present, they agreed that they needed to keep
their end of the wormhole open no matter what, just in case
Agent Brand made it back. They closed all the other ball pits
out in history, and Heathcliff adjusted the facial recognition
software on the Playground computers in hopes of spotting
their boss somewhere in time. But it gave them no word of
Brand or Ms. Holiday.

Still, there was good news. The present the children came
back to was changed for the better. The Playground was no
longer buried under concrete. President Lipton had never been
arrested and the NERDS organization was still a national secret.

Ruby hoped she would find things at home altered, too. As

she walked toward her house, her palms began to itch. She was allergic to uncertainty. What would she find beyond that door?

"Get in here out of the cold," her mother said, opening the door before she could even knock.

"Good news, sweetpea," her father said when she came through the door. "We found a hotel for everyone."

"And it's got a pool," Cousin Finn cheered as he raced into the hall.

The rest of the family followed. They were all there! Every single one!

"We'll be out of your hair in no time," Aunt Laura said.

"This hotel better have an elevator," Grandpa Saul said.

"Of course it has an elevator. What hotel doesn't have an elevator?" Grandpa Tom cried.

Predictably, a huge spat broke out with everyone bickering and talking at the same time.

"I'm going to order everything on the room service menu," Cousin Imogen said.

"Don't go," Ruby said.

"Huh?" her parents said simultaneously.

"I want you to stay," Ruby said.

"But sweetie, you're gonna have to sleep on top of the dryer," Grandma Rose said.

"No place I'd rather be. You're my family. As much as you

fight, it's a miracle we can all stand to be in the same room together. I want that miracle for this holiday."

"I call the bathtub!" said Grandma Tina.

That night, when everyone had found a space on the floor to sleep, Ruby caught the news. The lead story was that President Lipton had announced that he wasn't going to run for a second term. They cut to a press conference with him and his family. Tessa stood next to her mom, smiling.

"Being the president of this great nation has been a wonderful experience and a huge responsibility. I think we've gotten a lot done in the past three years, but that work has come at the expense of my family. Someone told me once that family has to come first, and she was right. So tonight I'm announcing that I will not seek a second term. I always wanted to be the president. I dreamed of serving this country. I imagined it was the best job in the world, but I already had the best job in the world."

Lipton took his wife and daughter in his arms and hugged them both as reporters charged forward with cameras and questions.

Ruby smiled. She and her team would have to keep a close eye on Tessa. She had upgrades and a nuclear-powered time machine, but Ruby hoped that the soon-to-be former First Daughter would no longer need it—or her second face.

38°53' N, 77°5' W

The next day, Heathcliff and Jackson walked to Heathcliff's parents' house.

"What if it doesn't work?" he asked. "The upgrades didn't exactly tell me how the nanobytes would get my family back."

"Then they'll just think you're some weird kid, and we'll go back to the drawing board," Jackson said. "Do you want me to go in with you?"

He shook his head.

"All right, Agent Hodges, good luck."

"'Agent'?"

"Ruby told me to tell you. She's going to need all the help she can get managing all the new recruits," he said. "Now get going. Oh, and good luck, buddy."

Heathcliff smiled. "Thanks . . . buddy."

He raced up the sidewalk and threw open the front door. "Mom! Dad!" he cried.

His mother was the first to appear. "Who in heavens are you?"

"Mom, it's me—Heathcliff. I'm home!"

"Thomas! Thomas, there's a strange kid breaking into our house," she cried.

Thomas came into view. He had a golf club in his hands and he was holding it threateningly. "Get out of our house!"

"Dad! Don't you know me?" Heathcliff asked.

"I'm calling the police," his mother said. She took out her phone and called 911. "If you don't want any more trouble, I'd leave right now."

Had the machine fooled him? Was it one of those super-dumb lessons he was supposed to learn? Like at the end of a book, when the fairy appears and tells him he had all the power he ever needed inside of him. That would be pretty lame, and he'd end up getting arrested.

"There's the siren," his father said.

Heathcliff panicked. They were going to take him away and his family would never know who he was. No! He couldn't let it end like that. They might not know him, but he needed them to know he was sorry for all the things he had done and that they were great parents and that all his mistakes had nothing to do with them. He needed them to know that their boy loved them dearly.

So he gave them a hug. His mom resisted at first, and his dad tried to shove him off, but Heathcliff hung on. He held the hug as long as possible.

He was still hugging them when the police came. They pulled him away and dragged him out to their car. They locked him in the backseat and went inside to talk to his parents. He was in big trouble, but he didn't care. Those hugs had felt good. He'd do it all over again in a second. Whatever they did to him, he would have those hugs.

A police officer returned with his parents in tow. He opened the car door and peered inside.

"Kid, get out of the car."

Heathcliff was confused but did as he was told. "Officer, I'm sorry. I didn't mean to scare these people. I just—"

"Heathcliff, shouldn't you be in school?" his mother asked.

"You called me Heathcliff!"

"Of course she did. That's your name," his father replied. "Are you feeling OK, son?"

"You called me 'son'!"

"Folks, what is going on?" the policeman asked. "I was called here for a breaking and entering."

"You must have the wrong house, officer," his mother said. "This is our son. He's in the sixth grade at Knowlton Middle School—though we have no idea why he's not there."

"I just missed you two. I wanted to come home," he said, and then he hugged them again.

39

Agent Brand stood in the teeth-chattering air outside a gas station in Novosibirsk, Siberia. A black car pulled up. He set down his oboe and eyed the car closely.

It was them.

He stood behind a trash barrel and waited. A tough, grizzled gangster got out of the car. Lars Corsica. Then the passenger-side door opened and a young woman stepped out. She was probably seventeen—just a kid, but blond and beautiful. It was her. He'd recognize that smile anywhere.

"First we get gas," Lars grunted in Russian. "Then we get married."

"Married?" the girl asked. There was uncertainty in her voice.

"Unless you want to go back home to your abusive parents?"

She shook her head.

"Then wait in the car."

The girl did as she was told, and Lars approached the gas station.

"Excuse me," Brand said in perfect Russian. "But could you tell me the time?"

Lars frowned and looked down at his watch. "Half past two."

"Then I'm right on time," Brand said as his fist caught the goon in the jaw. Lars fell over in the snow and lay very still. Brand bent down and took the car keys and the man's wallet, then hobbled over to the black sedan. He finished pumping the gas and got into the driver's seat next to the girl.

"Who are you?"

Brand smiled. "That's not important. What's important is that you know who *you* are. Your name is Viktoriya Deprankova, though there will be a time when people will know you by another name. That man out there—the one you're going to marry—he's going to steer you in a very ugly direction. I'm here to steer you the other way."

"Did my father send you?"

"No, I came because I care about you. A lot of people care about you."

"Are you crazy? I don't even know you."

Brand handed her the keys and got out of the car. "You will."

"Why are you helping me?"

"'Cause you're my holiday." He pointed west. "Drive down that road."

"Where will it take me?"

"Hopefully, America," he said.

Brand could tell the girl wasn't sure what to do, but after a moment she slid behind the wheel, rolled up the window, and drove off, leaving Lars behind.

Brand picked up his oboe and slipped it into his jacket. Then he went around the side of the gas station to a multicolored ball pit. He hopped inside and sank to the bottom, hoping that he had caused a ripple big enough to change the girl's life.

A second later he was in Marty Mozzarella's during a busy lunch rush. There were kids everywhere, and they stared as he floundered to get out of the ball pit.

"That's supposed to be for children, you know," a teenager in a giant mouse suit complained.

Brand growled, yanked the cable out of the pit, disconnected the control panel, and limped out of the restaurant.

The walk to Thomas Knowlton Middle School was a long one, but he completely forgot about his sore feet when he saw it. Hurriedly, he pushed the front door open and walked down the empty halls to a supply closet, where he found his familiar janitor's uniform. He pulled it on over his beat-up tuxedo then pressed the button that opened the tunnel to the Playground. A second later he dropped a mile into the earth.

The Playground looked like it always had. All the same faces were busy working on gadgets. Duncan and Flinch were lounging in their mission chairs while Jackson told them a joke, and Matilda was buzzing overhead, her inhalers blasting. Ruby was viewing a map of the world. The lunch lady, in his smock and hairnet, smiled and gave Brand a friendly wave.

"Look who's back!" Jackson shouted.

"You are seriously late for a mission update," Matilda said.

Brand smiled. "One of you is going to have to fill me in on what I missed."

"I can help you with that," Ruby said. "But first we have something very important to tell you."

Brand waved her off. "It can wait. Is she here?"

"Who?"

Brand's heart sank. "Never mind."

"Oh, you mean the new librarian?" Ruby said with a grin.

"Did someone call me?" came a voice. It had a thick Russian accent, but he would know it anywhere.

"Lisa," he said.

Benjamin floated between them. "Director, this is Agent Viktoriya Deprankova. She's just been assigned to the school. Her cover for the parents will be that of the school's librarian and media specialist."

He couldn't help but smile, and she smiled back at him.

"I made cookies," the woman said, offering him a plate of what looked like chocolate chip. Brand hesitantly took one.

One bite and he was sure he had cracked all his teeth. Yes, she was back.

Suddenly, an alert started blaring. Screens dropped from the ceiling and a dozen scientists raced to join the group.

"Oh, boy, looks like we've got trouble again. Baron von Baron has let loose his army of bionic ferrets. They're attacking the Taj Mahal," Duncan said.

"Scramble the team, Benjamin," Agent Brand said.

"Which team?" Heathcliff asked. He entered the room wearing a white lab coat and huge goggles.

"What do you mean, which team?"

"That's what I've been trying to tell you, boss," Ruby said. "We've got some new recruits."

Suddenly, hundreds of children walked into the control room. They saluted him and said, "Agents reporting for duty" in unison.

"I'm having a great time organizing them. I'll have a binder for you to look at when we get back. It's completely color-coded," Ruby said.

Brand smiled. "All right. It's time to get to work, NERDS. Let's go beat up some bad guys."

THE END

THERE WILL BE DAYS WHEN LIFE SEEMS HARD, WHEN THE BULLIES CORNER YOU OR HURT YOUR HEART, BUT THOSE DAYS WON'T LAST. THEY CAN'T LAST. SOME DAY SOON THE WORLD WILL LOOK FRESH AND FULL OF POSSIBILITIES AND YOUR DAYS OF BEING PICKED ON WILL END— JUST LIKE THIS STORY. AND THAT, MY FRIENDS, IS WHEN YOUR REAL STORY WILL TRULY BEGIN.
I PROMISE.

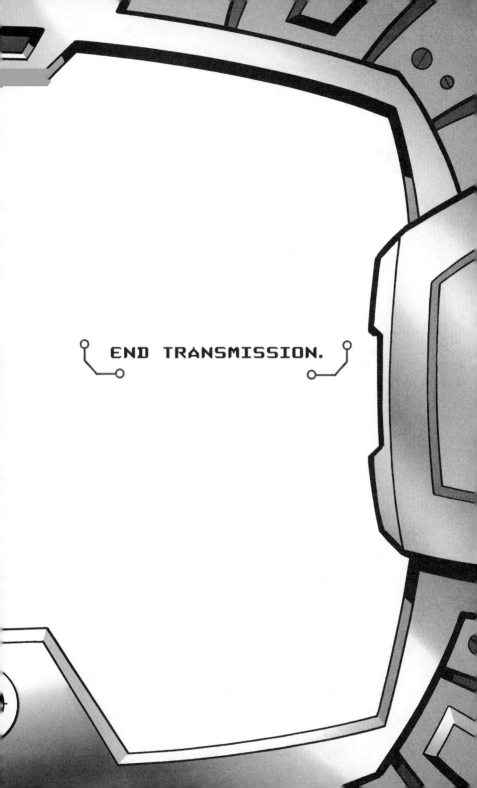

Acknowledgments

This series couldn't have happened without Susan Van Metre and Maggie Lehrman, whose tag-team editing proved that two heads are better than one. However, the true unsung hero of this series is Chad W. Beckerman, whose art design was inspired, fun, and cool. A special thanks to Ethen Beavers for coming on this ride to the end—thanks for your brilliant illustrations. Alison Fargis, both better half and agent, inspired every page. Thank you to everyone at Stonesong. Big props to

Jason Wells and his staff of super-publicists. A special thanks to fellow author and friend Julia DeViller for her insights into Ruby's Jewish/Christian upbringing. Thanks to Starbucks 11807 in Brooklyn and to Allie Bayles AND Topher Scotton. As always, my pal Joe Deasy for just being my pal, and to my boy, Finn, whose love of stories reminds me why I have the best job in the world.

Michael Buckley, a former member of NERDS, now spends his time writing. In addition to the top-secret file you are holding, Michael has written the *New York Times* bestselling Sisters Grimm series, which has been published in more than twenty languages. He has also created shows for Discovery Channel, Cartoon Network, Warner Bros., TLC, and Nickelodeon. He lives somewhere (if he told you where exactly, he'd have to kill you).

LEVEL 14
ACCESS GRANTED

BEGIN TRANSMISSION:

A conversation with Agent
Beanpole, a.k.a. Michael Buckley

Heathcliff changes a lot during the course of the series. Do you think he can really be trusted?

Well, the series touches on the idea of forgiveness and second chances. Jackson gets his, so why not Heathcliff? I think the heart of the problem is that he's just a hurt little boy who needs a hug . . . and maybe a straitjacket. Ha! I don't know if he can be trusted, but you can trust him to be interesting, for sure.

You put yourself in the last book. Is it odd being a character in your own book?

It was very odd because I didn't want anything bad to happen to me. When you write, if you write well, you have to make your characters struggle and suffer. That way the reader will care. But I'm a real person—I don't want to get beaten up by superpowered bullies or fall out of an airplane!

Not everyone has nanobytes to stop bullies. What are other ways kids can stand up for themselves?

The best thing you can do is get a grown-up involved in the problem. Talk to a teacher, a parent, a principal—anyone who can help. Make sure they know it's serious. If they don't help you, find someone else. You don't have to be bullied. It's not part of growing up. It's mean and you don't have to tolerate it.

The NERDS go through some embarrassing moments. Anything you'd like to share?

I could write a book about all my embarrassing moments. I remember one time I went swimming with my Cub Scout pack and somehow tore my swim shorts down the back. It was a huge hole and everyone saw it. Do the Cub Scouts have a "Dignity in the Face of Laughter" badge? Because I sure earned one!

How did you get the idea for the NERDS series?

I went to my high school reunion and saw how everyone had turned out. It seemed to me that the popular kids were sort of miserable and the nerds were having the best lives. I thought that was a secret worth spilling, especially to kids who can't see how amazing their lives will be. I thought about all the kids I grew up with, and the characters started popping into my head, demanding to be part of the story. Then I did a school visit at a place called Hammond Hill Elementary in North Augusta, South Carolina, with a lovely superteacher named Nikki Mock. I told the kids the idea, and we brainstormed the kinds of powers they might like to have if they were heroes. The rest is just nerdy history.

Were you a nerd in school?

Yeah. I didn't want to be one, and I would never have admitted it, but I was a disaster. What's funny now is when I talk to kids about the NERDS series, I'll ask them who thinks of himself as a nerd and the whole school will raise their hands. Being a nerd, being a little awkward and different, is actually a badge of courage for them. They're proud of it. Today's kids are far braver than I ever was. I wish I could have just accepted it. I spent far too much time trying to get people to think I was cool.

If you had nanobyte technology, what superpower would you have?

I would like to be able to make copies of myself so I could write all the stories that are in my head. I have a wild imagination . . . but never enough time or energy to write all of my ideas down. If I could just have fifteen or sixteen me's, you'd have some really fun stories to read!

This is the last book in the series. Will you miss writing about the NERDS?

I already miss them. I've been walking down the halls with these kids for almost five years. They're like old friends. But since they aren't real, I can't go on Facebook or whatever social media site is popular and see how they grew up. I just have to imagine it in my head—whom they marry, where they went to college, what jobs they have, if they're still heroes. I won't get to see them enjoying their day in the sun, but I smile knowing that it will happen. It happens that way for all nerds everywhere. Someday the future just shows up, and it's so bright.

END TRANSMISSION.

NOW THAT YOU'VE COMPLETED YOUR TRAINING AND LEARNED ALL THERE IS TO KNOW ABOUT THE NERDS, WHY NOT GO BACK TO THE BEGINNING AND READ AGAIN? WHO KNOWS WHAT YOU MIGHT DISCOVER . . .

This book was art directed and designed by Agent Chad W. Beckerman. The illustrations were created by Agent Ethen Beavers. The text is set in 12-point Adobe Garamond, a typeface based on those created in the sixteenth century by Claude Garamond. Garamond modeled his typefaces on ones created by Venetian printers at the end of the fifteenth century. The modern version used in this book was designed by Robert Slimbach, who studied Garamond's historic typefaces at the Plantin-Moretus Museum in Antwerp, Belgium.

COLLECT THE ENTIRE NERDS SERIES!

ALSO AVAILABLE AS ENHANCED EBOOKS, FEATURING EXCLUSIVE INTERACTIVE CONTENT!

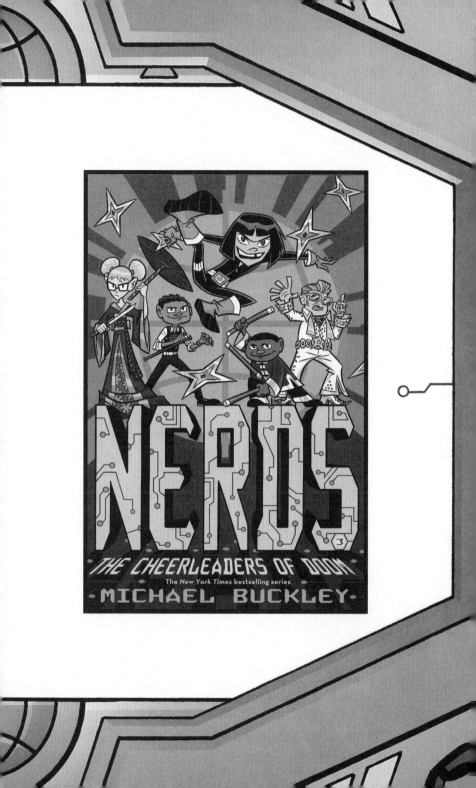

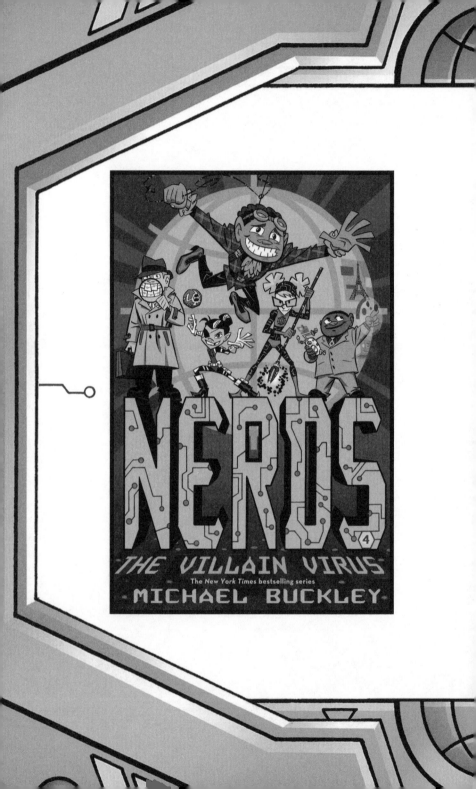

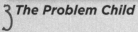